PENGUIN BOOKS

RAINTREE COUNTY

Ross Lockridge, Jr. was born April 25, 1914, in Bloomington, Indiana. The son of an historian father and a psychologist mother, he studied at Indiana University, the Sorbonne, and Harvard, always earning highest honors. From 1943 to 1946, he wrote *Raintree County*, while living in Boston with his wife and four children and teaching at Simmons College. He died a suicide at the age of thirty-three in his hometown on March 6, 1948, two months after his only novel was published to great critical and popular acclaim.

His son Larry searches for explanations in *Shade of the Raintree*, a biography of Ross Lockridge, Jr. published by Viking simultaneously with this new and corrected edition of *Raintree County*.

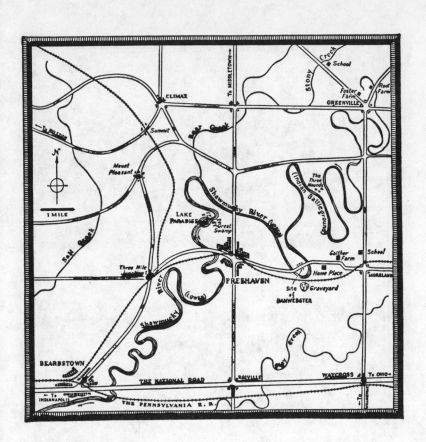

Raintree County

...which had no boundaries in time and space, where lurked musical and strange names and mythical and lost peoples, and which was itself only a name musical and strange.

ROSS LOCKRIDGE, Jr.

PENGUIN BOOKS

PENGUIN BOOKS
Published by the Penguin Group
Penguin Books USA Inc.,
375 Hudson Street,
New York, New York 10014, U.S.A.
Penguin Books Ltd, 27 Wrights Lane,
London W8 5TZ, England
Penguin Books Australia Ltd,
Ringwood, Victoria, Australia
Penguin Books Canada Ltd, 10 Alcorn Avenue,
Toronto, Ontario, Canada M4V 3B2
Penguin Books (N.Z.) Ltd, 182–190 Wairau Road,
Auckland 10, New Zealand

Penguin Books Ltd, Registered Offices:
Harmondsworth, Middlesex, England

First published in the United States of America by The Riverside Press
Cambridge, a Houghton Mifflin Company, 1948
Published in Penguin Books 1994

1   3   5   7   9   10   8   6   4   2

PUBLISHER'S NOTE
This is a work of fiction. Names, characters, places, and incidents
either are the product of the author's imagination or are used fictitiously,
and any resemblance to actual persons, living or dead,
events, or locales is entirely coincidental.

ISBN 0 14 02.3666 X
(CIP data available)

Printed in the United States of America

Except in the United States of America, this book is sold subject to
the condition that it shall not, by way of trade or otherwise, be lent,
re-sold, hired out, or otherwise circulated without the publisher's prior
consent in any form of binding or cover other than that in which it is
published and without a similar condition including this condition
being imposed on the subsequent purchaser.

For My Mother
ELSIE SHOCKLEY LOCKRIDGE
This book of lives, loves, and antiquities.

I wish to acknowledge the assistance of my wife, VERNICE BAKER LOCKRIDGE, whose devotion to this book over our joint seven-year period of unintermitted labor upon it was equal to my own. Without her, *Raintree County* would never have come into being.

ROSS LOCKRIDGE, JR.

Hard roads and wide will run through Raintree County.
You will hunt it on the map, and it won't be there.

For Raintree County is not the country of the perishable fact. It is the country of the enduring fiction. The clock in the Court House Tower on page five of the *Raintree County Atlas* is always fixed at nine o'clock, and it is summer and the days are long.

Raintree County is the story of a single day in which are imbedded a series of flashbacks. The chronologies printed here may assist the reader in understanding the structure of the novel. At the back of the book may be found a chronology of historical events with bearing on the story.

Chronology

of

A GREAT DAY

for

RAINTREE COUNTY

July 4, 1892

Morning

Dawn — *MR. JOHN WICKLIFF SHAWNESSY* awakens in the town of Waycross. (*page 3*)

6:00 — The Shawnessy family leaves Waycross by surrey.

6:45 — In the Court House Square of Freehaven, Mr. Shawnessy enters a Museum of Raintree County Antiquities.

7:45 — Across the site of the vanished town of Danwebster, Mr. Shawnessy carries a sickle and a box of cut flowers.

8:30 — Approaching the town of Moreland, *EVA* Alice Shawnessy reads the last page of *Barriers Burned Away*.

(*page 235*)

8:45 — Re-entering *THE GREAT ROAD OF THE REPUBLIC* in Waycross, Mr. Shawnessy is engulfed in wheels and faces. (*page 253*)

9:30 — Senator Garwood B. Jones arrives by special train in Waycross Station.

10:00 — Three men tip their chairs back against the General Store for a talk.

Evening

7:30 — On the porchswing at Mrs. Evelina Brown's mansion, an informal meeting of the Waycross Literary Society opens a discussion on *THE GOLDEN BOUGH.*

(*page 885*)

9:30 — Esther Root Shawnessy watches a cluster of torches approach the garden east of Waycross.

9:35 — From the tower of Mrs. Brown's mansion, Eva Alice Shawnessy beholds a celestial conflict.

10:50 — The last Fourth of July rocket explodes over Waycross.

Midnight — Professor Jerusalem Webster Stiles departs by train from Waycross Station.

CHRONOLOGICAL ORDER OF FLASHBACKS
(Page numbers show actual order in text.)

Raintree County

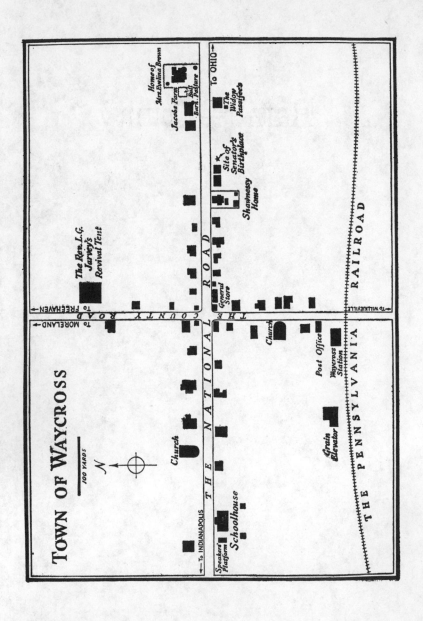

TOWN OF WAYCROSS

100 YARDS

N

To INDIANAPOLIS

To MORELAND

To FREEHAVEN

COUNTY ROAD

THE NATIONAL ROAD

THE ROAD

To OHIO

To WILKINSVILLE

Speakers Platform

Schoolhouse

Church

Church

Grain Elevator

Post Office

Waycross Station

The Rev. L. G. Jarvey's Revival Tent

General Store

Shawnessy Home

Site of Senator's Birthplace

Jacobs Farm

Home of Mrs. Ewlina Brown

Built Barn Pasture

The Widow Passifee's

THE PENNSYLVANIA RAILROAD

A Great Day

FOR RAINTREE COUNTY
(Epic Fragment from the *Free Enquirer*, July 4, 1892)

YES, SIR, here's the Glorious Fourth again. And here's our special Semicentennial Edition of the *Free Enquirer*, fifty pages crowded with memories of fifty years since we published the first copy of this newspaper in 1842. And, friends, what a half-century it has been! While the *Enquirer* has been growing from a little four-page weekly to a daily paper of twice the size, the population of these United States has quadrupled and the territory governed under the Institutions of Freedom has been extended from sea to shining sea. In those fifty years the Great West has been conquered, and the Frontier has been closed. The Union has been preserved in the bloodiest war of all time. The Black Man has been emancipated. Giant new industries have been created. The Golden Spike has been driven at Promontory Point, binding ocean to ocean in bands of steel. Free Education has been brought to the masses. Cities have blossomed from the desert. Inventions of all kinds, from telephones to electric lights, have put us in a world that Jules Verne himself couldn't have foreseen in 1842.

Folks, it has been an Era of Progress unexampled in the annals of mankind, and all of it has been made possible by the great doctrines on which this Republic was founded on July 4, 1776.

During those fifty years, we haven't exactly stood still here in Raintree County. Freehaven has grown from a little country town to a bustling city of ten thousand. The Old Court House of 1842 could be put into the court room of the present imposing edifice, one of the finest in the State of Indiana. And we challenge any section of comparable size in this Republic to show a more distinguished progeny of great men than our own little county has produced.

If anybody doubts the above statement, let him take a look at what is going on in the little town of Waycross down in good old Short-water Township. The eyes of the whole nation are fixed on that little rural community today. The celebration there to honor the home-coming of Senator Garwood B. Jones is a striking testimonial to the vitality of our democratic institutions. While we have often opposed Senator Jones on political grounds, we would be the last to diminish the lustre of his name or the distinction he has brought upon the county of his birth. We had hoped that the Senator would see fit to make his homecoming address here in the County Seat, but no one can doubt the political wisdom of Garwood's decision to speak in his birthplace, a town of two hundred inhabitants, as the opening move in his campaign for reelection. It's a dramatic gesture, and the Senior Senator from Indiana needs all his vote-winning sagacity, not only to defeat the rising tide of Populism this year, but to further his well-known ambition to achieve the Presidency in 1896.

Nor is the Senator the only nationally known figure in Waycross today. His friend and ours, another Raintree County boy, Mr. Cassius P. Carney, the famous multimillionaire, is expected to be there. And our own great war hero, General Jacob J. Jackson, is going to lead a march of G.A.R. veterans to point up the pension issue. There are rumors of other celebrities coming on the Senator's special train, and all in all it looks like the little town of Waycross will have dern near as many famous people in it today as Washington, D. C. If the celebrated Stanley set out to explore this dark continent tomorrow for the Greatest Living American, he could do worse than get off a train in Waycross to ask his famous question. . . .

Mr. John Wickliff Shawnessy

I PRESUME?

—Yes?

His voice was tentative as he looked for the woman who had spoken from the dusk of the little post office. The whole thing seemed vaguely implausible. A short while ago, he had left his house to take part in the welcoming exercises for the Senator, whose train was expected momentarily in the Waycross Station. Walking west on the National Road, he had joined the crowd that poured from three directions into the south arm of the cross formed by the County and National roads. A swollen tide of parasols and derby hats blurred and brightened around the Station. Except on Sundays, he had never seen over ten people at once along this street, and he had been afraid that he might not be able to reach the platform where he was to greet the Senator. Near the Station, the crowd had been so dense that he could hardly move. Women in dowdy summer gowns jockeyed his nervous loins. Citizens with gold fobs and heavy canes thrust, butted, cursed. A band blared fitfully. Firecrackers crumped under skirts of women, rumps of horses. From the struggling column of bodies, bared teeth and bulgy eyes stuck suddenly.

Then he had found himself looking into the glass doorpane of the Post Office, where his own face had looked back at him, youthfully innocent for his fifty-three years, brows lifted in discovery, long blue eyes narrowed in the sunlight, dark hair smouldering with inherent redness. He had just begun to smooth his big mustaches and adjust the poet's tie at his throat when the crowd shoved him against the door. It had opened abruptly, and stepping inside on a sudden impulse, he had heard the woman's question.

Now he shut the door, drowning the noise of the crowd to a confused murmur.

—I was expecting you, Johnny, the woman said in the same husky voice. Where have you been?

—I was just on my way to greet the Senator, he said. Is there—is there some mail for me?

He walked slowly toward the distribution window, where in the darkness a face was looking out at him.

—Some letters carved on stone, the voice said. The fragments of forgotten language. I take my pen in hand and seat myself——

The woman was lying on a stone slab that extended dimly into the space where the window usually was. She lay on her stomach, chin propped on hands. Her hair was a dark gold, unloosened. Her eyes were a great cat's, feminine, fountain-green, enigmatic. A dim smile curved her lips.

She was naked, her body palely flowing back from him in an attitude of languor.

He was disturbed by this unexpected, this triumphant nakedness. He was aroused to memory and desire by the stately back and generously sculptured flanks.

—How do you like my costume, Johnny? she asked, her voice tinged with mockery.

—Very becoming, he said.

Her husky laughter filled the room, echoing down the vague recess into which she lay. He hadn't noticed before that the slab was a stone couch, curling into huge paws under her head. He was trying to understand what her reappearance meant on this memorial day.

Watching him with wistful eyes, she had begun to bind up her hair, fastening it behind her ears with silver coins.

—What creature is it that in the morning of its life——

She paused and opened her left hand, color of the pallid stone on which she lay. The hand was excitingly feminine, though perhaps too broad, too fleshy for perfect beauty. She put her arm on his shoulder. Then with her hand gently plucking and pulling at the base of his neck, like one wishing to uproot a little tree without hurting it, she pressed his head down to hers. Reminding himself that she was an old friend of the family and perhaps even a relative, he was about to kiss her.

Just then she turned her face aside and handed him a rolled newspaper.

—Our Semicentennial Edition, dear, she said, with a special column devoted to the history of the County. The fragments from your own unfinished epic occupy a prominent place on page one. You'll find a picture of the authentic Raintree——

Opened, the paper was a parchment warm to the touch, engraved with a map of Raintree County so exquisitely made that the principal landmarks showed in relief with living colors. In the middle of the County, Paradise Lake was a pool of shimmering green. Its shore eastward where the river entered dissolved into the steaming substance of the Great Swamp. The roads crisscrossing on the flat earth were brown and gravelly. Tiny shiny carriages moved on the National Road, which, side by side with the Pennsylvania Railroad, cut across the County close to the southern border. Westward on the railroad, a darkly lovely little locomotive pulled a chain of coaches covered with patriotic bunting. The intersection at Waycross was dense with human faces. All over the County, the bladed corn swayed softly in the fields. In the Square of Freehaven, a mile and a half southeast of the lake, the Court House stood in a lawn of slender trees. A flag fluttered from the brave brick tower, and the four clock faces told the time of day. From the northeastern to the southwestern corner of the County, the Shawmucky River lay in loops of green, halved into upper and lower segments by the lake. On the road east from Freehaven two bridges spanned the upper river's great south loop, and in the halfcircle formed by the road and the river, relics of the vanished town of Danwebster lay in deep grass. Across the river was the graveyard, a mound of pale stones. And somewhat beyond the bridge on the south side of the road was the Old Home Place, a little collection of farmbuildings on a gentle hill, the ancestral Shawnessy home in Raintree County, where Mr. Shawnessy had been born fifty-three years before. So precise was the map that he could see the great rock halfsunk in the earth at the limit of the South Field.

He was certain that in the pattern of its lines and letters this map contained the answer to the old conundrum of his life in Raintree County. It was all warm and glowing with the secret he had sought for half a century. The words inscribed on the deep paper were dawnwords, each one disclosing the origin and essence of the thing named. But as he sought to read them, they dissolved into the substance of the map.

With a feeling suspended between erotic hunger and intellectual curiosity, he looked for the young woman. She was no longer lying on the stone couch. Her voice was passionate, musical, receding.

—Johnny! Tall one! Shakamak!

He could see her pale form turning over and over in a slow spiral floating away on green waters. From time to time, one hand rose beckoning while the other untwined her hair. The loose gold cord of her hair was at last all he saw of her, untwisting, prolonged in the water to a single shimmering thread.

Holding a branch of maize loaded with one ripe ear, he stood on the threshold of the door, about to lunge into the delirious crowd. The ceremonial day that he had spent a lifetime preparing, a web of faces and festive rites, trembled before him. The girls in their summer dresses were twirling their parasols and shouting hymen. The official starter of the Fourth of July Race was raising his pistol. A path was opening through the crowd to a platform erected in a distant square. Beyond, beside a sky-reflecting pool, he saw white pillars and a shrine. He heard a far voice calling. The sound was shrill, appealing, with a note of sadness. . . .

He awoke. The whistle of a train at the crossing had at last pressed its way into his sleep. It was early dawn. He lay in bed, among the glowing fragments of the dream. The dream had been vivid with the promise of adventure, consummation. He rewove its tantalizing web, contrasting it with the simple reality into which he had awakened.

His wife, Esther, eighteen years younger than he, lay beside him, her Indianblack hair screwed into curlpapers, her regular features composed by sleep into a look of stony, almost mournful serenity. In the next room slept the three children, Wesley, Eva, and Will, thirteen, twelve, and seven years old. The family slept in the two upstairs rooms of the plain white wooden house. There were four main rooms down—parlor, middle room, dining room, and kitchen, running in that order from front to back. A pumproom adjoined the kitchen, and a small spare bedroom was annexed to the dining room. A cellar with outside entrance was under the kitchen. A porch extended along the front and halfway down the east side of the house. The house was set well forward in a trimly kept yard, fenced in with white pickets in front and on the two sides. Almost against the house behind was a small frame building of two parts, smokehouse and woodshed. A path started at the backdoor and ran along a garden to the outhouse. At the rear of the lawn was a small barn. A narrow field planted in corn extended a hundred yards back to the railroad.

The town of Waycross, where Mr. Shawnessy had lived for two years, had an equally austere pattern. The business buildings were at the intersection of the roads—general store, barber shop, bank, feedstore, blacksmith shop. Half a hundred houses were scattered along the four arms of the cross. On the south arm were a church, the Post Office, and the Railroad Station. The Schoolhouse, where Mr. Shawnessy and his wife were the only teachers, was on the west arm. On the north arm was a huge tent where the Reverend Lloyd G. Jarvey had been conducting his Summer Revival Series. Among the dwellings on the east arm were the Shawnessy house, lying on the south side of the National Road, and the mansion of Mrs. Evelina Brown somewhat beyond the town proper.

In the naked pallor of dawn, Waycross seemed to him devoid of visual complexity, as if to reduce the problem of place to its basic ingredients. And Raintree County also aspired to spatial symmetry, being a perfect square twelve miles to the side. What could be more certain than the location of Raintree County, whose western border was sixty miles from Indianapolis and whose eastern border was fifty miles from the neighboring state of Ohio? And yet, the dream had left him with an uneasy feeling of being anchorless, adrift on an unknown substance. The formal map of Raintree County had been laid down like a mask on something formless, warm, recumbent, convolved with rivers, undulous with flowering hills, blurred with motion, green with life.

He mused upon this mingling of man's linear dream with the curved earth, couched in mystery like a sphinx.

Had the woman of his dream, whose face had been teasingly familiar, known the answer to this riddle? And what token could she have given him of himself, he who also escaped name and definition in his long journey through time, a traveller from dawn to darkness, and all at once a child, a man, an old man?

He should have asked this gracious lady about time past. He should have followed her beckoning hand down the mystic river of the years back to the gates of time, the beginning of himself. He should have traced a tangled thread to the source of a life on the breast of the land.

It was dawn on Raintree County, and in a little while he would have to yield himself to the ritual day. Past midnight, he had lain awake thinking about the big Fourth of July Program, in which, as principal of the local school and an old friend of the Senator, he had a leading responsibility. First he would drive to Freehaven, where he had some matters to see to before the Senator arrived. Despite the necessarily early hour of the trip, the whole family planned to go along as usual. On the way back, he would stop at the Danwebster Graveyard for his annual visit to the family lot. At nine-thirty the Senator's special train was due in Waycross, and the substance of Mr. Shawnessy's dream would be repeated—minus, no doubt, the interesting lady in the Post Office. Then he would entertain the Senator until the G.A.R. parade and banquet at twelve-thirty. The main program was planned for two-thirty, and after that he would see the Senator off at the Station. In the evening there was to be a lawn party sponsored by the Literary Society at the home of Mrs. Evelina Brown. It promised to be the most exciting day since his second marriage fourteen years ago.

He could still hear the thunder of the train on distant rails receding. Its passing echoed in the eastern valleys of his sleep. The lone shriek of it at the crossing had been like a calling of his name. The sound of it ebbing down gray lanes of dawn into the west was the lonely music of a century, awakening memories of himself and the Republic. He would lie awhile and chase a phantom of himself that was always passing on a road from east to west. He would hunt for the earliest mask of an elusive person, a forgotten child named Johnny, the father of a man.

What creature is it that in the morning of its life . . .

It was dawn now on Raintree County, and he would begin with things of the dawn. He would pursue awhile his ancient pastime of looking for the mystic shape of a life upon the land, the legend of a face of stone, a happy valley, an extinct republic, a memory of

ON THE MORNING OF ELECTION DAY
THE MOTHER AND THE LITTLE CHILD WERE WAITING

before the cabin. At the bottom of the yard, a rudely sculptured head stood on the gatepost by the road. Johnny had helped T. D. make it, and they called it Henry Clay, maybe because it had been made out of clay from the river bank.

—Henry Clay, T. D. had said, is the Greatest Living American.

T. D. had also said that Henry Clay was running for President, a matter of interest to Johnny, who for his age was considered a very fast runner himself.

The head on the gatepost had had an ugly, eyeless look when T. D. and Johnny first made it, but now at this distance it had an expression of greatness and distinction.

A few days ago when Johnny was in the yard by himself, a man had driven past in a covered wagon. He was a bearded man in a big hat, his wagon was pulled by two big oxen, it was all stuffed up with things, there was a thinfaced woman on the seat beside him, and a pretty little girl with vivid brown eyes kept peeping out of the wagon and shaking her pigtails at Johnny.

—Hello, son, the man said, stopping the wagon.

Big white teeth flashed through the thick bush of his beard.

—Hello, Mister.

—You look like a smart boy, son. Maybe you could tell me if this here is the road to Freehaven.

—Yes, sir, this here is it.

—How fer is it, son?

—You go on down the road, Johnny said, pointing west, and you git there after a while. They's a court house and a lots of people.

—Ain't he a smart boy! the man said, winking at his wife. Maybe you can tell me, son, what that there head is on the fence there.

—Henry Clay, Johnny said.

—Who's he?

—The Greatest Living American, Johnny said.

—You don't say, the man said. Who tole you so?

—T. D. did.

—Who's T. D.?

—My pa. He's a doctor and a preacher.

—Well, you go tell T. D. that that there head ain't Clay. It's mud. Anyhow it'll be mud after the Election.

—It ain't mud, Johnny said. It's clay. It was made out of clay, and it's Henry Clay.

—It's mud, dad burn it! the man said. You tell your pappy somethin' else. You tell him a man passed said Henry Clay *ain't* the Greatest Livin' American. He's nothin' but a goddern Whig protectionist. Can you say that?

—Yessir. A goddern Whig protectionist.

The man roared, and the woman said something to him. The man leaned out again.

—You tell your pa you saw a man, and he told you the Greatest Livin' American was James K. Polk. Yessiree, James K. Polk is the man that's goin' to win that election. James K. Polk.

The man was motioning big and violent with a whip.

—James K. Polk. The Lone Star Republic and the Oregon Trail. Can you say that, son?

—The Lone Star Republic and the Oregon Trail, Johnny recited.

—Listen to him say that, the man said. How old are you, son?

—Five.

—You're a smart boy, son. You'll amount to somethin' some day. Don't fergit that slogan. James K. Polk is the man that'll win the Election, and he'll make Clay's name mud.

—It ain't mud, Johnny said. We got it down along the river. Mud's black. This here's red, and it's clay.

—O.K., son, the man said. But all the same, don't fergit to tell your pa what I said. The Oregon Trail. That's where I'm a-headin' right now, and if your pappy was half a man, he'd be a-goin' there with me to settle out there and git that land fer America instead of votin' fer Harry Clay and Protection.

The man made his whip lash over the backs of the oxen.

—Oregon, here we come!

As the oxen pulled away, the girl with the pigtails leaned from the wagon and waved her hand. She waved a long time, and Johnny waved back.

It seemed to him then that he had always been a small boy who stood beside a road and waved to people going west.

Later when he had told his father about it, T. D. had laughed and said to his mother,

—I wonder what they were doing off the main road.

—Where is the Lone Star Republic and the Oregon Trail? Johnny had asked.

His father told him something about them.

—Are there Indians out there?

—Yes, I reckon there are, T. D. said.

The Indians used to live right around the Home Place before T. D. and Ellen Shawnessy had come there in 1820. The Indians were naked and had red skins, and they lived in tepees, and they killed and scalped you with tomahawks. They were marvellous people, and they had lived all over America before the pioneers came and made the stumps. Now all the Indians had gone out West, where the man in the covered wagon was heading.

Next to the Indians, the most interesting people were probably the Negroes. Men would get together in front rooms and around the Court House at Freehaven, shake fists, spit tobacco, and talk in loud voices about the Negroes and the Election and Polk and Clay and Texas and the West.

The Negroes were black slaves in the South. It was a bad thing to keep them slaves and make them work. Johnny had walked through the South Field once and had gone a long way back hoping to see a Negro. He never did see one.

But that same day he kept on going and wound around back north until he crossed a road and came out at the Gaither farm. Nell Gaither was playing in the orchard under an appletree. She was a thin, serious girl with long golden hair, big blue-green eyes, and a freckled nose. She had a quiet, grave way of talking in contrast with Johnny's older sisters, who were very giggly and loud.

—You're Johnny Shawnessy, she said.

—Yes, I am.

—I'm Nell.

—Is the river back of your house?

—Yes. I'll show you.

The river was a big mystery to Johnny. Now he and Nell walked a piece and pushed through some trees and came right out at the

edge of the river. It was wide and pale green, and it had a cold green odor. He and Nell had played a long time by the river building little mud and stick huts. They both waded out looking for crawdads and frogs. Johnny forgot all about the time until he noticed that long shadows were falling on the river.

—Your folks'll be after you, Johnny, Nell said.

—Let 'em, Johnny said.

You had to run away from home to have a good time like that.

When he started down the road that evening, he ran into a lot of people, and they all rushed at him and grabbed him and took him home.

Later his mother had come home on a horse, all hot and dusty and her dark red hair in strings down her face. She began to cry when she saw Johnny in the front yard surrounded by people. She hugged him very hard and kept saying, Thank God! and laughing and crying at the same time. Johnny cried too from sheer excitement. It appeared that he had been lost and found again. People said that his mother had ridden all over Raintree County looking for him.

—Poor Ellen! people said. Johnny, you pretty near killed your poor mother.

They never let him go back and play along the river again with Nell because it was too much fun.

That was when he learned that he was a person of great importance and that his exact location in Raintree County was a matter of intense concern to everyone.

Ellen Shawnessy, his mother, was short and slight. Though not pretty, she had a young girlish look. Her hair, dark with glints of red like Johnny's, was entirely ungrayed. Johnny was the last of her nine children, four boys and five girls. Two of the girls had died in an epidemic that swept through Raintree County in the early forties, and they lay beneath two stones with letters on them in the Danwebster Graveyard, across the river from the board church where T. D. preached.

—What is a great man, Mamma? Johnny asked as they waited in front of the cabin for T. D.

—A great man is somebody everyone looks up to. He's a good man who does things for other people.

—Like Pa?

Ellen Shawnessy smiled. Her smile was like Johnny's, quick and affectionate. More often than not she smiled for no other reason than that she felt animated and happy.

—Well, T. D. is a mighty good man, she said, and he's smart too. But usually a great man is a wellknown man. That is, he's famous.

Johnny's father, T. D. Shawnessy, preached and wrote poetry and delivered babies and made sick people well. He was very tall and thin, and his head looking down at Johnny from a great height always nodded blondly and benignly and smiled confidently and spoke very hopefully of God and the future.

—I aim to be a great man, Johnny said. Is God a great man?

—God isn't exactly a man, Ellen Shawnessy said. He's—well—he's just God. He's a divine being. That is, he's greater than any human being.

God was the biggest puzzle of all to Johnny. He had begun to worry about God during the summer when the Millerites were camping out in Raintree County. When the family would be riding down the road, they would see at night the bonfires burning on a distant hill.

—There's them plaguey Millerites, T. D. would say.

The Millerites were out there on the hill waiting for the End of the World. T. D. said that in his opinion it wouldn't come for quite a while yet.

In those days, God was a whitebearded giant who lived up in Heaven but had a sneaky way of being everywhere else at the same time. He could do anything he wanted and just waited around for you to make a mistake, whereupon he would land on you and whop you good. Johnny used to wonder if it would do any good to go out and hunt for God. But God was just as scarce as the Indians and the Negroes in Raintree County. There were times when Johnny wondered if God was just a big story, the kind that big people were always telling little people.

Later on that day when T. D. came home, they all got into the wagon, the older ones sitting on chairs in the wagon bed, and went into Freehaven. There was a big crowd around the Court House Square, people talking loud and waving banners. Later the older children took Johnny down to the Polls. Johnny looked around for some tall sticks, but it turned out that the Polls was a place where a lot of people were trying to put papers into a box.

Several big barrels were hoisted on sawhorses and wedged into the crotches of trees, and men kept going over and turning on the taps and getting brown stuff out of the barrels. Johnny got lost from the other children for a while and was swept up in a crowd of people marching and chanting:

> —Vote, vote, for James K. Polk!
> The Lone Star Republic and the Oregon Trail!

Johnny marched and chanted too, until T. D. spied him and striding into the middle of the parade carried him off.

—Don't you know them's Democrats, John? he said.

A lot of men went around swatting people on the back and laughing fiercely. T. D. put a paper in the ballot box. Things got louder as the night came on. Bonfires burned on the Court House Square. The family had a big feed in the wagon, and after that Johnny slipped off into the crowd with his brother Ezekiel, who was two years older than he and a lot bigger. They watched some men hitting each other and yelling things about God, Polk, and Clay over in front of the Saloon. A man was knocked down and had his coat torn off. A woman came up shrieking and grabbed at the man lying on the sidewalk, so that Johnny didn't see how he could get up if he wanted to. Zeke disappeared for a while, and when he turned up again, he was grinning all over his face and said he had just beaten up on a goddern kid that admitted he was a Democrat. Zeke showed his knuckles all skinned and bruised.

Late at night, the family started back to the Home Place in the wagon. Johnny lay for a long time awake with his head in his mother's lap, looking up at the stars. He hunted the heavens until he saw one big star low in the west. He thought it might be the Lone Star. Somewhere out there in the Far West, under the night and the shining stars and across the Great Plains, was the Lone Star Republic and the Oregon Trail. Right now maybe the little girl with the pigtails was out there.

Johnny Shawnessy decided that some day when he was big enough to go away from home by himself, he would go over and get Nell Gaither, and they would get into a big covered wagon and go down and find the National Pike, and they would ride off together toward those big plains and those far western mountains beneath the shining stars, where the land was fair and free, where the Indians lived in tepees, and the streams were full of fish, in the country called the United States of America, which was somewhere in Raintree County.

For in those days, he didn't very well understand the boundaries of Raintree County or of his own life. Raintree County was simply the place where people lived, it was the earth, and you might go anywhere and never leave it. He had heard people talk of a time when there was no Raintree County. He used to think back and back to see if he could remember such a time, and he would come to a place where all his memories fading reached a green wall of summer. Sometimes he would attempt to cross that wall, vaguely wondering at the murmurous world beyond it from which his being had been ferried up some summer long ago to be deposited in Raintree County. He had some dim intuitions and memories of it, all drenched in green and gold. Nameless, and neither child nor man, he had lived in a beautiful garden where stately trees dripped flowers on the ground. And somehow that life was longer than all the rest of his life together. But long ago that summer of wordless forms had been lost to him, or rather the forms had been subtly changed and hidden by a veil of words.

Now in the still night, Johnny Shawnessy was carried in a wagon over the dark earth of Raintree County, which had no boundaries in time and space, where lurked musical and strange names and mythical and lost peoples, and which was itself only a name musical and strange.

And lying in his mother's arms, he went to sleep and dreamed that he was riding in a ribbed and canvascovered wagon down a road at night toward a lone star palely shining over fields of summer.

—Look there! everyone said. The Greatest Living American!

In the red far light of the star, he saw an immense face of clay, and he and all the other people were running for President as fast as they could go. So in the still night

HE DREAMED A FAIR YOUNG

DREAM OF

GOING

WESTWARD, the National Road pursued its way, a streak of straightness to the flat horizon. As the surrey approached the intersection, Mr. Shawnessy was thinking of his dream. Although he had since risen, dressed, eaten breakfast, and set out for Freehaven, he was still haunted by the riddle of a naked woman in the Waycross Post Office. The dream had distilled the conundrum of his life into one image, delightful and disturbing.

She had reminded him of his plural being. He had presented to her Mr. Shawnessy, a dutiful citizen of the Republic calling for his mail. She had addressed herself to mr. shawnessy, a faunlike hero, poised on the verge of festive adventures.

Mr. Shawnessy, meet mr. shawnessy. Hail and farewell! Farewell and hail!

Just now, the majuscular twin, Mr. Shawnessy, was sitting upright in the front seat of the surrey beside his wife, Esther, while the three children, Wesley, Eva, and Will, occupied the back seat. It was a characteristic Mr. Shawnessy attitude, for Mr. Shawnessy was eminently a family man and a respectable citizen. When he called at the Waycross Post Office later in the morning, he wouldn't find a naked woman on a stone. Instead he would receive the *Indianapolis News-Historian* from a fat-faced functionary named Bob.

Only the adventurous twin, mr. shawnessy, could achieve naked women in post offices. For mr. shawnessy was a lower-case person, disowning all proper names, including his own, and many other proprieties. Yet it was convenient to call him mr. shawnessy since he was always moving in and out of Mr. Shawnessy with pleasant alacrity, using his obliging companion as a kind of depot for incessant arrivals and departures. In fact, mr. shawnessy used Mr. Shawnessy as a straw man, a large comfortable mask that he had spent a lifetime adapting for public performances.

Mr. Shawnessy, the straw man, was now driving the family westward through Waycross, an inseparable part of the Shawnessy landscape. At the intersection, he would turn due north, being a creature bounded by severe alignments.

He was bounded by the Nineteenth Century and knew only one way to escape—by living his way out moment by moment.

He was bounded by a box, the County, inside a box, the State, inside a box, the Nation, inside a box inside a box inside a box.

He was sartorially bounded by his one good suit, a cloth of light black wool, newly pressed for the day, a white shirt, a black poet's tie, knobtoed black shoes, dark soft hat. A hundred dollars would not have persuaded him to walk down the street of Waycross in an Elizabethan doublet, a woman's bonnet, or naked.

He was linguistically bounded by the English language, which he spoke with a Hoosier accent, though, when he pleased, with precision, wit, and eloquence.

He was morally bounded by a certain code of right and wrong that Moses had brought down from Sinai into Raintree County. He had a way of lingering wistfully on thresholds without crossing.

He was a completely legal person. On April 23, 1839, his birth had been accomplished from an inkwell in the Raintree County Court House. His marriage to Esther Root in 1878 had achieved a whole column of print on the first page of the Raintree County *Free Enquirer*. The children who occupied the back seat of his surrey on trips around the County were what was known as legitimate. He enjoyed certain rights of citizenship under the Constitution of the United States and certain inalienable rights under the Declaration of Independence, among them, Life, Liberty, and the Pursuit of Happiness.

He was a creature of amazing certainties. He had his infallible Saturdays and his relentless Mondays. He almost never went to bed in the middle of the night or rose at noon. And every year the Fourth of July came and bestowed on him firecrackers, patriotic programs, and a drive with the family to the middle of Raintree County where he placed some flowers on a grave.

He lived in a precariously poised world of taboos, pomps, and games called American Society—with no spectacular triumphs, it is true, but in a manner to inspire confidence and respect. In fact he was one of the priests of the temple, being responsible for teaching the communion to others, for he had spent a lifetime instructing the young of Raintree County in what is known as the rudiments of education.

In a world convulsed with war, famine, industrial unrest, and public and private vice, Mr. Shawnessy was a citizen of the American Republic, living quietly on the National Road of life where it intersected with Raintree County, and tacitly involved in a confused course of human events that the newspapers and people in general agreed to call American History.

The versatile twin, mr. shawnessy, on the other hand, was a fugitive from boundaries. No sooner did he appear to be caught in a definition than he somehow turned inside out to include the includer. He was always pressing beyond the confines of himself, yet could never go anywhere that wasn't himself.

His seeming foothold in the Nineteenth Century was illusory. His face peered furtively from a frieze of the Parthenon, passed in mob scenes in the reign of Justinian, crossed with crowds on Brooklyn Ferry ever so many centuries hence.

His landscape was an infinitely potential number of Raintree Counties past, present, and to be. He was always arriving in train stations from parts unknown to meet himself departing for unknown parts.

In him, the word and the thing almost rejoined each other at the source. His words were dreams of things; his dreams were things of words.

He had a way of joyfully crossing the thresholds at which Mr. Shawnessy lingered.

He had no legal existence whatsoever. His birth was recorded, if anywhere, in the first chapter of Genesis and his death was foreseen only in Revelation. Eve was his mother, his daughter, and his wife, and he was the citizen of a republic that never was on sea or land.

Of course, his being was all tangled up in that of Mr. Shawnessy. The two were always colliding with each other as Mr. Shawnessy went his ritual way through conversations and thoroughfares, and mr. shawnessy carried on his eternal vagabondage through a vast reserve of memories and dreams. But even in dreams the carefree twin had to do devotion in strange ways to Raintree County and its gods. It was clearly the whim of mr. shawnessy to prepare a naked woman on a stone slab in the Post Office, but it was Mr. Shawnessy who timidly asked for a newspaper, trying his best to adapt himself and his puritan conscience to the bizarre world of his twin.

Yet doubtless there was really only one John Wickliff Shawnessy, one Raintree County, one Republic, one riddle with plural masks. That was what the young woman with the catlike eyes had meant by the half-given line from a legend of antiquity:

What creature is it that in the morning of its life . . .

Mr. Shawnessy had made the turn north onto the County Road. But the insouciant twin had kept the westward bias.

Westward the star of empire. Westward the Great Companion takes his way. Shirt open at the neck, broad hat pushed back on matted, vital hair, he walks the boulevards of westward cities, crosses the wide windrippled plains, ferries the Mississippi, and strikes out strongly through the sagebrush mesas. He climbs the sunblaze summits of the Rockies, descends deep passes to the Golden Shore.

> O, Californy!
> That's the place for me!
> I'm off for . . .

Firecrackers crumped in backyards. A smell of patriotism tinged the early morning air.

—How long before we get back, Papa? Wesley asked.

—About nine o'clock. We have to be back by then.

—What yuh readin', Eva? little Will asked.

— Book, Eva muttered, absorbed.

—I want to be back in time for the service, Esther Shawnessy said, as the surrey passed the Revival Tent.

—We'll be in time, Mr. Shawnessy said. We won't be stopping in Freehaven long. And I only mean to leave a few flowers at Mamma's grave.

—Papa, what's Senator Jones look like? Will asked.

—I haven't seen him for twenty years. When I last saw him, he was a big heavyset man, broadshouldered, deepchested, with blue eyes, dark brown hair, and a voice like a bull.

—What's General Jackson like?

—The General looks like a fighting man. Of course, he's pretty old now, but in his prime he was a fine figure of a man.

—Will he have his uniform on?

—I imagine so.

—Will he have a sword?

—A dress sword maybe.

—O boy! Jiminy! A sword! How many wars did he fight in?

—Just two. The Mexican War and the Civil War.

—The Mexican War. When was that?

—Eighteen forty-six to eighteen forty-eight. I was about your age then, Will.

Are you Johnny Shawnessy? Yes, sir. Can you read, son? Yes, sir. Well, read this then.

—Did they have a Fourth of July when you were a boy, Papa?

—Sure.

—Did they have firecrackers and things?

—Big ones.

Bang! Forward, boys, all along the line! Kill the damn greasers! Westward the star of empire.

The Fourth of July was the memory of a lone white rocket rising in the purple sky above a town in Raintree County long ago. The rocket burst and feathered into burning spray and floated softly on the fields of night. The Fourth of July was the memory of a new republic, a bloody babe of destiny, waiting to be filled with soul. The Fourth of July was a war on sunbaked plains, a fighting in the high passes and in California. It was the pasteboard red of fire-crackers, the blue of armies charging stiffranked in steel engravings, the white of flowers flung by girls in summer dresses for the boys who fought at Buena Vista. It was the fury and the fighting heart of a young republic, fledgling of the nations, conceived in battle and confirmed in battle. It was a lone star rising in the east and westward tending. It was a million faces pressing westward, the harshvoiced dreamers of a strange, disordered dream.

Mr. Shawnessy jingled the reins over President's back, passing the last houses of Waycross. Meanwhile mr. shawnessy roamed on other roads. There had been a wagon shrugging down a road to westward years ago. It had gone on for days creaking across the vast plain. Where were all the days of the travellers in that wagon?

But those days had passed, and the girl with the pigtails had grown up, no doubt had married and borne children. The burly charioteer of the westward sun, who had driven his oxdrawn car through Johnny Shawnessy's life, had died long ago, and the wagon itself was ribs of weathering wood in a far lone valley of the West.

A small boy had wandered out into the morning of America and down far ways seeking the Lone Star Republic and the Oregon Trail. A small boy had dreamed forever westward, and the dream had drawn a visible mark across the earth. But the boy had never gone that way. He had only dreamed it.

He saw the face of a girl fading among the vehicular tangle of the years. All the evenings of a life in the West dyed the sunset peaks with purple—the lost years ebbed with waning voices in the cuts where the little trains passed, crying. Yes, he had been fated to stay after all, chosen for a task that called for more than ordinary strength. He and only he had stood on the earth of Raintree County in an early summer dawn and had had that deep vision of the Republic, the passionate, westward dream.

> I had a dream the other night,
> When . . .

were long in the hot weather that summer, and the world of Raintree County seemed fixed around him like paintings on a wall. Then one day a horse thundered up the road from Freehaven and into the yard of the Home Place, and a young man got off. He had long blond hair under a broad hat.

—This where Doctor Shawnessy lives?

—Yes, sir, Johnny said.

He and the man went to the Office behind the house.

—What's the trouble, son? T. D. said.

—Why, my wife's gonna have a baby, sir, the man said. We got into this here town of Danwebster over here last night, and she was took sudden and before her time. Some fellers in town said as how you was the best baby doctor around here. I'd be mighty obliged to git some help for my wife.

While T. D. was getting his medical kit, Ellen came out and talked with the young man, who said that he was from Tennessee and was on his way to California. He and his wife had left the National Pike intending to stop with friends in Middletown, but the woman had come down unexpectedly with labor pains. It was her first baby.

Johnny was pleased when he was permitted to go along with his mother and father to Danwebster.

—It's the house right aside of the General Store, the man said, getting up on his horse. Name is Alec Doniphant.

While they were driving to Danwebster, Ellen said,

—Courteous young feller. It must be awful hard on 'em having their first baby on the road thisaway. There's so many of 'em these days. Anything to get out West.

When they got to Danwebster, T. D. and Ellen went into the house with Mr. Doniphant. There were several men sitting on a bench in front of the General Store. Just as Johnny got settled on the bench, he heard a low sound from the house, musical like a mouth rounded. The men on the bench listened without turning their heads.

—She ain't a-hollerin' loud enough yet, a man said.

He was a fat old man everyone called Grampa Peters. Those days, he always seemed to be sitting on the bench before the General Store in Danwebster. A Democrat of the old Jacksonian breed, he was reported to have Southern sympathies and was the only person in town who received a newspaper regularly.

—I seen them come in last night, a thin man said. She was in considerable pain then and kept a-cryin' out all night.

There was another low moan from the house.

—She'll have to bear down harder than that, Grampa Peters said. She ain't puttin' herself into it yet. She'll have to make up her mind to have that baby.

A cry of pain lay suddenly on the quiet street.

—That's the first real loud one I've heard her give, Grampa Peters said. That was a good loud one.

His flesh stirred a little as if pleasantly goaded by this fierce contact with life. He fumbled around in a coat pocket and drew out a newspaper.

—Son, can you read?

—Yes, sir, Johnny said.

—I heard you could, Grampa Peters said. They say you read as good as a grown person. Well, I want you to read me somethin' here. I fergot my specs.

Grampa Peters spread out a copy of a newspaper. At the top it said

THE INDIANA COURIER

—Read that there righthand colyum for me, Grampa Peters said.

Johnny read outloud how the Whig Nominating Convention meeting on June 7 had nominated General Zachary Taylor for the Presidency. While he was reading, T. D. and Mr. Doniphant came out of the house.

—How's she comin'? Grampa Peters asked.

—She's pretty little and of course it's her first one, T. D. said absently. But she's young and strong, and I take a hopeful view of the situation. After all, having a baby is the most natural thing in the world.

—I hope it comes soon, young Mr. Doniphant said.

—I think it'll be a while, T. D. said. My wife's going to stay with her. You look fagged out, young feller. You better relax awhile.

—Git us that there banjo of yours, the thin man said, and play us some music.

—I reckon it might take my mind off of it, the young man said, and he went back of the house.

—What about it, T. D.? Grampa Peters said, when Mr. Doniphant was gone.

—It's a hard case, T. D. said. She hasn't really got anywhere with it yet, and she's very narrow. There isn't anything to do but wait. However, as I said before——

His voice trailed off.

—What you got there, John?

—Newspaper.

—The boy was just readin' it to us, the thin man said. He's a bright boy.

—How'd you learn to read, son? Grampa Peters said.

—I learned at school.

—John learned at this here school in Danwebster, T. D. said. He can read anything. What's in the news these days? I haven't seen a paper for mighty near a month.

—I see where your danged Whigs nominated old Blood and Thunder, Grampa Peters said.

—Yes, so I hear, T. D. said. Well, I guess he'd make a good President.

—Maybe that's what we need, a military man, the thin man said. The country's so all tore up. Winnin' the war pretty near wrecked us.

—Pretty near wrecked us! Grampa Peters snorted. What are you talkin' about, boy? Some folks don't reason things out. Who made this glorious victory possible and added all this here new land to the Republic? The Democratic Administration—that's who.

—Couldn't have done it, hadn't of been fer ole Zach Taylor whippin' the damn greasers, the thin man said.

—What's Taylor's stand on the slavery question? T. D. said.

—Probly, he ain't got no stand, Grampa Peters said. Call it a straddle rather.

Johnny read some more from the paper. It appeared that General Taylor had avoided the slavery question. There was a good deal in the paper about the old veteran of many a hardfought campaign who had personally inspired his stalwart troops on the windy plains of Buena Vista.

Johnny was glad that General Zachary Taylor was going to be the Whig candidate for President because he was the Greatest Living American.

Zachary Taylor was a rugged, whitehaired old man standing in the middle of a wall engraving. Stiff ranks of soldiers dressed in blue advanced across a plain through volleys of bounding cannonballs. In the background of the picture a darkskinned horde, color of the earth, dissolved in flight.

The War with Mexico was a pageant of names that made your flesh tingle. The names were Rio Grande, Monterey, Buena Vista, Vera Cruz, Cerro Gordo, Cherubusco, Molino del Rey, Chapultepec, Mexico City. The names were Zachary Taylor, Winfield Scott, John C. Frémont. The names were the Santa Fe Trail, Oregon, New Mexico, and California. The names were color of the sun on deserts and treeless mountains, color of buckskin breeches and blue coats, streaming South and West in a perpetual Fourth of July.

The Mexican War was a memory of orators, long hair combed back lush behind their ears, frock coats flapping, standing on the platform in the Court House Square, raising and dropping their arms and bellowing the names of battles and heroes. Johnny remembered the recent Fourth in Freehaven, when the County had turned out to welcome back its boys who had fought in Mexico. Marching at their head was the young hero, Captain Jake Jackson, who had distinguished himself in the attack on Chapultepec and been three times wounded as he led his men over impregnable defenses. The girls of Raintree County had flung flowers on the marching soldiers.

Johnny wished the men in front of the General Store would talk more about the real war, but instead, as usual, they talked about slavery.

Grampa Peters kept saying that the best thing to do was just to leave the whole question alone and not get the South all excited about it and that the territories to be carved out of the new land would settle the question of slavery for themselves. He said there never would have been all this fuss and fidget if it hadn't been for the Wilmot Proviso. The thin man said that the South was all for throwing over the Missouri Compromise and that they never would be satisfied to let California come in as a free state.

—Damn them! the thin man said, getting excited, as people always did sooner or later when they talked about the new lands and slavery, that's what they fought the damn war for—slavery.

T. D. was inclined to take a hopeful view of the situation.

—It was destiny, he said. We was going in that direction.

Mr. Doniphant came back, carrying his banjo. He sat down and sang some songs in a soft whanging voice, and while he was singing, Ellen came out of the house to listen, and some other people gathered around.

—Sing that one you sang last night, Grampa Peters said.

Mr. Doniphant sang:

> —I come from Alabama
>   With my banjo on my knee,
> I'se gwine to Louisiana,
>   My true love for to see.
> It rained all day the night I left;
>   The weather it was dry.
> The sun so hot, I froze to death,
>   Susanna, don't you cry.

The chorus went:

> —O, Susanna,
>   Do not cry for me;
> I come from Alabama
>   With my banjo on my knee.

The best verse was the second:

> —I had a dream the other night,
>   When everything was still;
> I thought I saw Susanna dear,
>   A-comin' down the hill.

> The buckwheat cake was in her mouth,
> The tear was in her eye.
> Says I, I'se comin' from the south,
> Susanna, don't you cry.

—That's a good one, Grampa Peters said.

They had him sing it again.

—Where'd you learn it? T. D. said. I don't recollect ever hearing it before.

—O, I picked it up in a camp of folks over in Ohio. We had a different way of singin' it too that they made up around there. They was some of 'em singin' it thisaway:

> —O, Californy!
> That's the place for me!
> I'm off for Sacramento
> With my washbowl on my knee.

—Reckon you intend to git some gold out there, eh, son? Grampa Peters said.

—Well, sir, Mr. Doniphant said. I didn't know if all them stories about there bein' gold there was true. Most people just said they heerd it from somebody else. I thought I'd git me some land. If they is gold to be got, maybe I could git some of it too. I ain't worryin' none about it. All I want is to git out there.

—What d'yuh think about this here slavery question, son? Grampa Peters said. Do you think they'd ought to keep slavery out of them new lands?

Young Mr. Doniphant strummed softly on his banjo.

—Well, he said softly, I don't know how you folks feel about it around here. Me and the folks I been travellin' with goin' West don't want no slave labor to compete with in the new lands.

—But have they a constitutional right to prohibit it? Grampa Peters said. That's the question. There ain't any right under the Constitution to prohibit it. That's all I say.

—Maybe they ain't, the young man said. But I don't figger there'll be any slavery in the new lands.

He strummed softly on the banjo, humming,

> —O, Californy!
> There's the land for me.

I've tooken quite a journey from
My home in Tennessee.

—If we keep slavery from spreading, T. D. said, it will die natural of its own accord. Slavery's a wrong, and nothing can make it right. I take a more or less hope——

Something bit and tore the mildly spoken words. Young Mr. Doniphant stood up, ashamed and scared.

—D'yuh think——

—She's all right, T. D. said. It's natural. The pains are getting sharper.

—No good baby was ever got without a lot of yellin', Grampa Peters said.

Ellen and some other women went back into the house.

—Take it easy, son, T. D. said. This may go on all day.

—By the way, T. D., Grampa Peters said, could you let me have another bottle of them pokeberry bitters sometime? My stummick's been actin' up on me agin. Sometimes I think I can't hardly stand it.

Mr. Doniphant sat down slowly and kept picking nervously at the banjo and humming,

—O, Californy!
That's the place for me!

—What route do you figure on takin' to git out there? the thin man said.

—Why, I don't know yet. I aim to take the safest.

—After what happened to them Donners, Grampa Peters said, I reckon you can't be too careful. I wonder if you ain't goin' to have to winter over somewhere before you try it.

—Maybe so, the young man said.

—Have you seen any Mormons along the way? T. D. said.

—Not as I know of. They say the Mormons has all gone out and got them a place out there somewheres.

—I seen a book, Grampa Peters said, and it had a picture in it of a Mormon goin' to bed with his wives. That there bed was simply swarmin' with women pullin' each other's hair and feedin' babies.

—One woman's more'n enough fer me, the thin man said. They'd ought to take and burn all them Mormons at the stake.

Those days, people were always going West. Johnny had heard it said that along the National Pike there was a wagon every hour regular and at times a whole train. Nothing could stop the people from going West. They had babies along the way, like Mr. and Mrs. Doniphant. They died in the snow on the mountains and ate each other to keep from starving, like the Donners. They had a scad of wives in one bed like the Mormons. Most of them were slightly crazy some way. But they kept right on going. Perhaps it had something to do with the sun that made an arc day after day above the National Pike. Johnny thought of the western land under the far setting of the sun, wide plains in purple evening through which on softly thundering hooves the buffalo herds were running, he thought of Indians, riding swift ponies toward the flanks of purple mountains, wagontrains streaming thinly westward, he thought of shining rivers, green slopes, blue ocean on the distant shore of evening.

Those days, Johnny thought much of gold, Indians, great rivers, buffalo, and men who carried guns. Before the war, the West was a vagueness, a direction, a place of few names that belonged mostly to someone else. Now, however, it was good to think that the Nation extended from sea to shining sea.

—Here's an interesting item, T. D. said, shaking the newspaper. It tells here how they laid the cornerstone for the Washington Monument.

—I wonder will they ever git that thing built, Grampa Peters said. Seems to me I've heard talk of it for a long time now.

—O, I guess they'll get it built some——

A cry cut across T. D.'s sentence. This time it lasted longer than usual, and Mr. Doniphant got up and went into the house.

—Now that's what I call a good loud one, Grampa Peters said. Sounds like the real business, T. D.

—How do you stand listenin' to 'em all the time, T. D.? Just this one's drivin' me crazy, the thin man said. But I suppose you git use to it.

—I never will get use to it, T. D. said. But the Lord requires it of Woman for her Sin, and so it must be.

—I guess it must hurt 'em somethin' awful, the thin man said.

Grampa Peters belched complacently.

—By God, I got to git me another bottle a them bitters.

Each time the woman cried, Johnny wanted to crawl off somewhere and hide. His pleasant landscape of Raintree County revolved dizzily, running with rivers of blood. Life was not what he had supposed it to be. When his mother appeared at the door, he turned his face away. He and all his brothers and sisters had entered life by an incredible wound inflicted on that slight beloved form. This was what the word 'woman' really meant.

—Daniel Webster, Grampa Peters was saying, much as I oppose him in most questions, has the right idea about this whole slavery thing. Stand upon the Constitution, and all will be well.

In those days, people were always standing on the Constitution. The Constitution was like the Bible. When you appealed to the Constitution, you had made the ultimate appeal. If you could quote the Constitution to support your argument, you had quoted God. People who quoted the Constitution always did so solemnly and as if that finished the matter. The majority of arguments ended by each man appealing to the Constitution, and the man who did it oftenest and in the loudest voice was adjudged the winner.

Not that anyone ever really won.

It seemed as though Grampa Peters' remark about the Constitution set the argument going again. More men gathered around, and as the woman in the house cried more often, the men talked more loudly and profanely about slavery, westward expansion, and presidential candidates. There appeared to be a contest between the men before the General Store and the woman in the house to see which could get the best of a furious debate in which the two contestants were determined to ignore each other. But to Johnny, only the cry of pain was real. It filled up the street. It drew a bloodred streak across the day. And at last it compelled silence and respect.

After a particularly loud cry, Ellen came to the door and said,

—You better come now, T. D.

—Must be the breakin' of the waters, Grampa Peters said.

—O, my God! a woman's voice cried from the house. O, dear God!

—That's all right, honey, Ellen Shawnessy was heard saying. Go right on and holler, honey. Just holler as loud as you want to, if it helps.

The men sat cowed. Johnny hated them and himself. He hated

especially Grampa Peters. He hated the portly bulk of Grampa Peters, squatting majestically before the General Store; he hated the male complacency of Grampa Peters, which never had to be torn open and rent by such an anguish, the trousered fatness of Grampa Peters, who only sat before the General Store on his big dumb behind and made words about politics while life shrieked in an upstairs room. He hated all men in the person of Grampa Peters, because men caused this awful thing to happen and then could do nothing about it.

After the screaming had gone on for a while, the men began to curse softly.

—Well, Jesus God, I wish she'd hurry up and git it over with.

—Goddammit! Grampa Peters said once. I don't remember my wife yelled that loud, though God and Jesus knows she always yelled loud enough.

—They sure git the raw end of things, the thin man said.

After a particularly frightful yell,

—Well, Jeeeeeeeeeesus God in Heaven, Dear Lord! said Grampa Peters, git rid of it, sister!

The men began to act as though they were being abused in some way. As for Johnny, each time the shrieking came, the skin of his face drew tight, his chest heaved, tears came to his eyes, he wanted to scream, roll on the ground, and yell with laughter. The desire to laugh became so strong that he had to get up and walk away. He went to the big wagon that was in back of the house where Mr. Doniphant had gone for the banjo. He got behind the wagon and tried to laugh, but instead he was sobbing. Apparently that was what he had been wanting to do.

After a while, the shrieking stopped and was followed by a series of moans and then a silence. The men got up and stood looking at the house. Johnny felt strangely calm. He dried his eyes and walked back to the road and stood with the men.

There was a new sound, which was like an echo of the other, a piping, insistent little echo, helpless and shameless as the other. But after that sound began, the other sound never did return.

The men in front of the General Store began to smile, at first a little sheepishly, then broadly.

—By God, listen to that little pipsqueak howl a hisn.

—That ain't no pipsqueak howl. He's got a good loud yell fer a baby.

—He ought to have, if he takes after his maw.

After a while, the door opened, and Ellen Shawnessy came out.

—They want you all to come in and see it, she said.

—I reckon they'd *better* leave us see it, said Grampa Peters. I never worked harder to have a baby in my life.

The men all removed their hats and walked sheepishly into the house. Johnny brought up the rear. In a room upstairs, a woman was lying on the bed. Her cheeks were flushed, and her hair was all strung around on the pillow. She was looking at something lying on her arm. Her husband was standing beside the bed looking at it too.

It was a little hairless monkey with a scalded skin, the ugliest thing Johnny had ever seen.

—It's a boy, said Mr. Doniphant tentatively.

—It's a *fine* boy, Grampa Peters said, lying magnificently.

The mother only lay looking at the baby. The baby was yelling again, and T. D. said,

—A perfect baby. The beginnings of a fine family, my boy.

Some of the men hit Mr. Doniphant solidly between the shoulders, and others pumped his hand. He looked bewildered and kept saying,

—Thank ye, sir, thank ye.

—Well, Missus, Grampa Peters said, how do you feel?

—All right, said the woman on the bed. I'm sorry if I caused y'all trouble by carryin' on so. I never knowed what it'd be like.

All of them lied, saying they didn't notice a thing, and anyway it didn't bother them the least bit.

—What you goin' to call it, Missus? Grampa Peters asked.

—Well, the young woman said very slowly, looking at it, we was aimin' to call it, iffen it was a boy, Zachary Taylor Doniphant, but I done change my mind, and my husband and I would like to give him the name of this kind gentleman here who help us out and maybe save my life and the baby's.

—O, I assure you—— T. D. started to say.

—No, sir, Mr. Doniphant said, we talked about it while you was all out of the room just now, and we're a-goin' to christen 'im Timothy Shawnessy Doniphant, if the doctor don't mind.

—Mind! T. D. said. I would be delighted. But I assure you——

Johnny thought it was a terrible insult to his father because the baby was a monstrous-looking object, but T. D. seemed to be delighted.

—T. D., one of the women said, I think that calls for a little prayer.

T. D. blew his nose and put his head down. The baby kept on crying.

—Dear Father in Heaven, T. D. said, these good young people have come a long way across the great continent of America and have suffered many hardships. So far Your kind providence has been upon them. We ask You now to continue to favor them with the benign light of Your countenance and take a hopeful view of their future, far-wandering across the land. May this little child that is this day born unto them live and prosper in the far land to which they are journeying. Dear Lord, preserve him and his father and his mother in the trials that await them. May they reach that far-off beautiful land of California and may they find all of their desires fulfilled until they arrive as all of us must, after much wandering, on that Golden Shore where there is no distinction between here and hereafter. We ask it, Lord, in Jesus' name. Amen.

Outside, everyone made a little contribution for the new baby, and T. D., who had already donated his services, gave two dollars. The baby was yelling again when they went in to give the money to the Doniphants. One thing you could say for it: it had a lot of life in it.

Johnny was very quiet until they were on their way home. Then he found that he was humming a song:

--O, Susanna,
Do not cry for me.

—I wish I could get the words to that song, Ellen said. How much do you remember, Johnny?

Johnny started in, and it turned out that he knew the whole song.

—It pays to have a good memory, T. D. said. With your mind for remembering things, John, you ought to go far.

The tune had a fine gaiety, but the words filled Johnny Shawnessy with delicious sadness, and the name Susanna haunted him even into his sleep, for that night he dreamed that he was hunting through the

Court House Square for a mysterious woman, whose stately name he couldn't remember. Meanwhile the Square darkened; people were rushing by him in wagons going west.

—It's the breaking of the waters, they said solemnly.

And indeed he could see the cold waters of the Shawmucky rising in the cornfields. He himself, trying to escape, wandered all night through familiar landscapes. They had an empty, joyless look

LIKE PAINTINGS ON A WALL

OR PICTURES

IN

AN
ILLUSTRATED HISTORICAL
ATLAS
OF
RAINTREE COUNTY
INDIANA
1875

In the back seat of the surrey little Will had the book open.

—Who is that lady above the door, Papa?

He pushed the book over into Mr. Shawnessy's lap. The title was stamped in gold on a black clothbound cover, eighteen by fifteen inches. The *Atlas* was an inch deep, corners and spine reinforced in tooled black leather. The fullpage lithograph of the Court House showed a rectangular brick and stone building. A tall tower set into the west end contained the Main Entrance, an American flag stood stiff out from the peak of the tower, and two clock faces visible in the sloped roof read nine o'clock. Two ladies, bustled, bearing parasols, walked on symmetrical paths of the court house lawn. Over the Main Entrance a draperied woman stood in a niche, blindfolded, leaning on a sheathèd sword, holding bronze scales.

—Justice, Mr. Shawnessy said.

—What are those things in her hands?

—Scales. To measure the exact difference between right and wrong.

—Why do they call it an atlas? Will asked.

—An atlas, Mr. Shawnessy said, is a book with maps—pictures of the earth. In the old Greek stories, a giant named Atlas held the world on his shoulders.

—Hercules came and held the world for him once, Wesley said, while Atlas went to the Garden of the Hesperides and got the golden apples for Hercules.

—What did Hercules want with the apples? Will asked.

—It was one of his twelve labors. And when Atlas came back, he just laughed at Hercules and said he was going to leave Hercules there holding the world forever. He didn't want to take the world back.

—You can't exactly blame him, Mr. Shawnessy said.

—But, Wesley said, Hercules played a trick on him. He fooled Atlas into taking the world back just long enough so he could fix his lion skin on his shoulders to keep the world from chafing them. And as soon as Atlas had the world back on his shoulders, Hercules just laughed at Atlas and took the apples and beat it, leaving Atlas to hold the world.

—He isn't still holding it, is he? Will asked.

—No, of course he isn't, Wesley said. It's just a Greek myth.

The *Illustrated Historical Atlas of Raintree County* was not, however, just a myth. It was a very substantial piece of work. A Chicago firm had sent its own compilers, surveyors, and delineators to make a verbal and pictorial record of Raintree County. Fifteen years ago Mr. Shawnessy had bought a copy of the *Atlas* for ten dollars and put it on the parlor table with the Family Bible and the Photograph Album. The *Atlas* was printed on paper of excellent quality, great grainy sheets, some forty-eight in all. There was an illustrated title-page, colored fullpage maps of the County and each of its twelve townships, and smaller maps of the principal communities, including Waycross. At the back were unfolding maps of Indiana, the United States, and the Eastern and Western Hemispheres. The reading matter provided a history of the County, statistical tables, and descriptions of churches, eminent public buildings, newspapers, and schools. Ten whole pages were given over to a list of over five hundred prominent citizens, each of whom had given satisfactory proof of prestige and good taste by subscribing to the *Atlas* in advance.

The name Shawnessy, J. W. appeared on page 44.

The *Atlas* was remarkable for its illustrations, fullpage lithographs of the New Court House, Freehaven's leading hotel, the south side of the Square; and half a hundred pictures—some fullpage and some two and four to the page—of Raintree County homes, mostly farms.

Into the faintly golden texture of the great soft sheets, an unknown artist had touched the earth of Raintree County with a sensitive pencil. In the sketches of farm homes, the principal building was seen as from a slight elevation so as to include a generous setting of outbuildings and the land around. Walks, lanes, roads, forests, gardens, pastures, cornfields appeared in accurate perspective. People played croquet on lawns; children skipped ropes, rolled hoops, pulled wagons; families passed in surreys, spring wagons, buggies; mare and colt scampered in the pasture; the great bull passively grazed behind the barn; the farmer engaged in his characteristic occupations—feeding, mowing, raking, plowing.

The earth had the effect of being a massy substance continuous under all traces of humanity. Through page after page, this earth of Raintree County appeared in an unvaried summer morning, radiant and precise to a depth of miles, until sky touched horizon with a frieze of soft clouds.

One played with the idea that the artist had been a gifted young man forced to hack for a living but leaving the stamp of genius even on his routine assignments.

—How come you're taking the *Atlas* to town, Papa? Wesley asked.

—What's that? O, to exchange it for one at the Museum, which is slightly different. They can use mine while I have theirs.

—How is the one at the Museum different? Wesley asked.

—It's an earlier edition, Mr. Shawnessy said evasively. What's Eva reading?

He didn't listen to the answer. He was thinking of Senator Jones's letter in his pocket and the quaint mission that he was undertaking to Freehaven.

The letter had come to him a week before. Everyone who knew the Senator well, knew that he had two distinct styles—sacred and profane. His informal letters to close friends favored the second vein.

Dear John:
    . . . By the way, on top of all your painful responsibilities for the success of my homecoming, I want to pile one more that ought to be a pure joy to you.
    As you know, I haven't been back to the County for twenty years, but I still have good contacts there and keep up pretty well. Now, here's a story I picked up in '75 when I received a copy of a Raintree County Atlas. I was told that the artist who drew the pictures for it was on his last job for the company before getting the axe. It seems

he fancied himself a Raphael without a patron and was going nutty from so much hack work. Anyway, he got even with his firm and the world in general for years of artistic frustration by letting his imagination run hogwild on the plates he did for the Atlas. So when old Waldo Mays, who founded and ran the Historical Museum and was the leading spirit in getting the Atlas commissioned, received his advance copy, he took one look and beat it the hell up to Chicago, where he demanded the plates and had them altered or destroyed in his presence. All the rest of the subscription was castrated, including your copy and mine.

Meanwhile old Waldo kept the unique copy under lock and key in the Museum and never let anyone see it. Harve Watkins, who gave me the story, says Waldo kept hinting that the damage hadn't been all cleaned up, so that people kept scurrying to their Atlases to see if they could see anything. My own copy is ragged.

I've heard several hot tips about Waldo's unique copy, to wit: A lovely dame is standing in her pelt, ankledeep in the river under the railroad trestle on the titlepage. The lady going into the dry goods store on the south side of the Square, page 37, is stark naked, except for a parasol. On page 65, Bob Ray's prize bull, Mr. Jocko the Strong, blue ribbon at the State Fair in '74, is pictured showing prizewinning form in an intimate domestic scene. On page 53, Titian's Venus and Adonis are romping in the forest background. Adam and Eve are under an apple tree on page 57. A pair of country lovers are surprised in a haystack on page 17. The fountain in the front yard of John J. Jubal's palatial home in Beardstown features an ithyphallic Aztec god instead of a cast-iron triton. The sign reading Burke House on Freehaven's leading hotel has been altered to something more pungent. And Jesus Christ surrounded by the Twelve Apostles is getting ready to jump to Zion from the observation platform of the house on page 61. You can see the possibilities.

Now, I've been using this story for years with great éclat in the smokefilled rooms of the Nation's Capital, Washington, D. C. I adapt it for the company. It's good for lusty laughter at the stag banquet, and in a daintier version it fetches a giggle from the most cultivated females in Washington.

I'm sure there's some truth in it because I once wrote old Waldo myself in my best senatorial style, stating that I understood he had in his possession a unique copy of the Atlas containing some interesting variations, and as I was collecting books of all kinds on the old home county out of a sentimental interest, I would be glad to buy his copy— and he could name the price.

The old bastard wrote back that the variations to which I referred were of such a profane character that he had sworn never to allow the copy to get into the hands of another human being, where it might expose a character less staunchly fortified than his own, to overwhelming temptations. He said that he planned to destroy the book before his death and delayed now only because the presence of it in his museum brought hundreds of folks every year who bent bug-eyed over the glass case in his private office, where he kept the book locked up and covers closed. He said he considered this an excellent training in self-denial, not to say that it encouraged people to explore the Museum and its other treasures (all those goddamned stinking stuffed possums and Indian skulls).

That Atlas has become an obsession with me. I have the same feeling about it that a collector would have for the famous Satan's Bible with the misprint in the seventh commandment or a hitherto undiscovered Shakespeare play published with the author's face engraved from life in the frontispiece and an autobiographical preface.

Now, just last week I got word from Harve that old Waldo was found stiff and stone-cold at six in the morning on the front steps of the Museum with his key in the lock. Apparently, feeling that his hour had come, he'd staggered down in the dead of the night to get that book and destroy it. And they say his niece by marriage and only heir (who's been East and got married and widowed) was visiting the old man in his last illness and immediately took over the estate and the Museum lock, stock, and barrel and closed it up for adjustments.

In other words, John, that cussed book is in the hands of a woman, young, pretty they say, and therefore impressionable—instead of an old he-frump who has been lusting over it in secret for seventeen years.

Someone is going to get hold of that book now—and fast. If I were in the County, I'd be willing to bet my chances for the Presidency in '96 that I'd get access to the lady and the book in a matter of hours. But since I can't do it, my first thought is you. We all know, John, that where a skirt is involved, you carry a golden key.

Sprout, I'm personally counting on you to put the hex on that woman and get that book and have it in Waycross when I arrive. My letter to her is already in the mail, blazing the trail, and I leave the rest up to you. I'll personally lay out a cold hundred dollars for the privilege of adding that book to my private collection of prints by the old masters.

Of course, I didn't give my birthyell yesterday, and I know the whole thing may have been just a figment of the old man's mind. We all know that Waldo has been off his nut ever since he cracked his marbles on a wagontongue as a boy on his father's farm. But I don't want to go to my grave without satisfying my curiosity as to what that two-bit Michelangelo did to Raintree County.

By the way, John, not a word on this subject where it might diminish that splendid image of decorum which the hoi polloi entertain for a U. S. Senator. Of course, in the right quarters it will give my character that touch of humanity which woos the beauteous ballot to the box—and after all, this is an Election Year. . . .

Cordially yours,

GARWOOD B. JONES

Mr. Shawnessy had in his pocket another letter received two days before.

My dear Mr. Shawnessy,

Your kind note in hand, I hasten to reply. The book of which you speak and in which Senator Jones has expressed an interest is in my possession. Apparently my revered uncle placed a great value on it, but I would be glad to see you and talk with you about it.

I am opening the Museum for Independence Day, as many people like to visit. If you come early, before seven, as you suggest, I will meet you there on the Fourth.

By the way, you are wrong—I remember you quite well. As a little girl of ten, I was a doting protégée of yours. You trained me and some other girls for a patriotic pageant on the Court House lawn in 1868. I had the part of the Productive Institutions and wore a skirt made out of corn husks which came off halfway through my speech.

So you see, you are not forgotten after all. Remember me kindly to your family.

Sincerely,

PERSEPHONE R. MAYS

The surrey had turned west at Moreland and was approaching the Old Home Place. Granite boulders were strewn on the earth here, negligent droppings of the great ice sheet whose southernmost rim had lain on Raintree County aeons before, leaving its load of alien rocks and glacial dirt.

Fleshed with loam, tufted with groves, and dense with corn, the earth swam beneath him and away to distant summer. The sky built a vault pillared with far clouds over the floor of Raintree County.

What made the earth of Raintree County? Who holds up the earth? *What creature is it that in the morning of its life . . .*

Man made an atlas for the earth and tried to get a lasting place among the Prominent Citizens. With straight lines—ranks of corn, telegraph poles, rectangular walls—he tried to overcome its feminine evasions. Across its mapflattened face, devoid of contour, he drew the unwavering legends of his names. But he had never caught the naked goddess in his net.

Mr. John Atlas Shawnessy had reluctantly taken the world back on his shoulders, releasing his heroic twin, Mr. John Hercules Shawnessy, who ran off bearing a branch of golden apples. With fleet thighs, he fled up and down the corridors of a mythical Raintree County. He laughed. His gold hair hung long on his shoulders. He had held the world for a little while, or rather he had drawn it with a sensitive pencil and had made a delightful legend of it, had sketched forbidden beauty into a puritan landscape, achieved Acropolis in the Court House Square, Shakespeare at the County Fair, Venus risen from the Shawmucky, Eden in an apple orchard.

Take back the world a minute while I adjust my lion skin. There, you poor benighted bonehead, you can keep it. Did you build yourself a respectable world and bound yourself beneath it, friend, and call it Raintree County? Well, I will tell you what it is—your Raintree County—to reward you for plucking me these golden and forbidden apples.

I will give you back the world neatly bound in tooled leather and black cloth by the firm of Jackson, Higgs, and Company, Lakeside Building, Corner Clark and Adams Streets, Chicago, but with a few special additions of my own. As the anonymous artist sent down from headquarters, I don't hesitate to say that I have improved a little on the work of God in making you this legendary Raintree County. The universe never did sufficiently reward me for my intuitive perspectives.

Ladies and gentlemen, let's take off on our conducted tour of Raintree County. Look sharp! There's more naked here than meets the eye. These sentimental landscapes are full of sly gods. And from the back of our book, we unveil you the earth, our lady of the stately hemispheres. Look sharp, ladies and gentlemen! This little magic world within a world is strewn with the memories of all mankind.

—There's the Old Home Place, Wesley said. Look, they've been cutting clover in the South Field.

A plain white farmhouse, surrounded by weathered outbuildings, stood on a slight elevation leftward of the road. Scarred and strange, it lay on the immemorial way to Freehaven; and passing it, Mr. Shawnessy passed again through an invisible great gate and into the garden of a Hesperian memory, seeking

FABULOUS AND FORGOTTEN SECRET
WAS WRITTEN IN A LOST LANGUAGE UPON THE EARTH

of Raintree County. This he had known from the beginning, and he had known too that the secret was for him to unriddle; he alone could one day find the answer. For this secret was not only the secret of the earth in which he lived but also the secret of himself and what he was. Who and what are you, little manchild? Whence have you come and whither are you going? What are you doing upon this ancient, stream-divided earth?

Many devious paths seemed to lead backward to the secret.

There was the secret of the County's origin and naming. The County seemed to Johnny an eternal thing, and yet only some twenty years before his birth, it had been an indivisible part of central Indiana, then a new State, admitted to the Union in 1816. In 1818, the central region was opened up for white settlement, and counties were created by an act of the state legislature meeting in the new capital, Indianapolis. After that, the settlers came, mostly Scotch-Irish and English stock from the coastal states. They poured into the southeastern corner of the County by way of the National Pike, among them young T. D. Shawnessy and his wife, Ellen.

The way in which the County got its name was a subject involved in mystery. The first state legislature had called it after a hero of the Revolution, but later, when a legal county government had been formed and a site selected for a county seat, a petition was accepted for changing the name to Raintree County. Clearly enough, a sentiment had grown up in the County for the new name, but exactly why was never fully understood.

According to a popular legend, the earliest settlers found a ragged preacher wandering in the neighborhood of a lake in the middle of the County. He told them that in his youth he had had a vision of Heaven in which he beheld a green land full of fruitbearing trees and pleasant waters and had gone seeking for its earthly counterpart through the wilderness of America, carrying with him the seed of an oriental tree never before planted in America. Now he had found, as he believed, the land of his vision.

—Lo! I have sowed the seed, he cried. The Raintree will blossom in the western earth. The tree of life will drop its golden fruit in the new earthly Paradise.

The mad preacher had worked so strongly on the imagination of the first settlers around Freehaven that they began to refer to the neighborhood, a little facetiously, as the Land of the Raintree. From this source came at length the names Paradise Lake and Raintree County.

Some people insisted that the preacher had been no other than the celebrated John Chapman, better known as Johnny Appleseed. A ragged, quaint, beloved form, he had spent his life travelling through the pioneer West, planting apple orchards in the wilderness and preaching a Swedenborgian gospel of the teeming, sacred earth. If the man who planted the Raintree was Johnny Appleseed, then it seemed likely that the seed he planted was only apple seed. Perhaps he had merely established one of his famous tree nurseries somewhere in what was to become Raintree County.

At any rate, no one had ever found the eponymous tree of Raintree County, and after a passage of years people in general began to assume that there was no such tree as a Raintree.

Then something happened that seemed strangely to confirm the legend of the County's naming.

In the year 1826, the Scotch philanthropist Robert Owen founded New Harmony on the Wabash River in southern Indiana. Down the Ohio and up the Wabash came a Boatload of Knowledge—scientists, artists, and educators imported from the East and from overseas to found a New Moral World in the western wilderness. People were invited to come and join a paradise regained by innate human goodness. The noble experiment lasted two years and collapsed in the usual picturesque wreckage of innate human selfishness and inefficiency. But many gifted people remained and fostered an interest in science and art so much advanced for the place and the period that New Harmony came to be known as the Athens of the West. Among the New Harmonians were students of natural science, and it was one of these who brought to New Harmony the seeds of an exotic tree, which he planted by the gate of his house. This tree, bearing the scientific name of Koelreuteria paniculata, had been called the Golden Raintree in its native China. From these parent seeds the Golden Raintree—or the Gate Tree, as it was commonly known in Indiana—spread all over New Harmony and more slowly through other parts of the State. It bore no fruit in the popular meaning of the word, but in late June or early July the mature trees, which seldom grew taller than twenty or thirty feet, bloomed with a delicate yellow flower and dropped a rain of yellow pollendust and petals.

Thus, by chance, the State of Indiana did acquire a mysterious seedling of Asia, a true Raintree. But for a long time this tree flourished only in a little town in the southwestern corner of the State, while the county named for such a tree had not a single specimen within its boundaries, as far as anyone knew.

Not that anyone in Raintree County was ever much disturbed by the paradox. No one ever challenged New Harmony's claim to having introduced the Asiatic Raintree to America. Scarcely anyone knew about the gate trees of New Harmony, and no one except one or two garrulous gaffers and Johnny Shawnessy cared how the County got its name anyway. The earth had taken back one of its legends—that was all.

Nothing would remain at last except the name itself, itself a legend beautiful and talismanic, a sound of magic and of recollection, a phrase of music and of strangeness—Raintree County.

Johnny Shawnessy never doubted the truth of the legend. He felt sure that a wondrous tree grew in secret somewhere in the County. People might have passed beside it a hundred times and never realized that it was the tree planted by the fabulous preacher, whose name was also Johnny.

Johnny Shawnessy used to imagine that someday he would be walking in a wild, rarely visited part of the County and in the late afternoon would come upon a tree rising jetlike from the earth and spreading to a fountain spray of dense leaves, among which was a fruit of delectable flavor. He used to imagine the stately trunk of the tree and the clean isolation of it from the other trees of the forest. Or perhaps it was standing lonely in a field of grass. Once Johnny had asked T. D. where such a tree could grow unseen in the County, and T. D. said,

—They's a regular wilderness around Paradise Lake, especially
where the Shawmucky flows into it. Folks call it the Great Swamp.
Why, a man went in there once and never come out again. There
could be a whole slew of such trees in there and no one ever know
about them.

Johnny felt that there was only one tree, one sacred trunk standing in the druid silence of woodlands in the middle County. Someday, perhaps he would find that tree and thus become the hero of the
County, the Alexander who cut the Gordian knot, the Hercules who
obtained the Golden Apples of the Hesperides, the Oedipus who
solved the Riddle of the Sphinx.

The secret of the tree was blended strangely with the whole secret
of his life and the mystery from which he had sprung.

In T. D.'s Office, the little building behind the house, there hung
a big picture of a tree with a black printed legend beneath:

THE LEAVES OF THE TREE WERE FOR
THE HEALING OF THE NATIONS

When he was very young, Johnny had thought this tree had something to do with the mythical tree of Raintree County. Later he understood why T. D. had the picture.

The Office was nearly as old as the log cabin which had been the
original Shawnessy Home in Raintree County. A shrine of memories, it had its own peculiar incense. If from all the herbs of Raintree County a scent had been distilled, that quintessential fragrance
would have been the scent of T. D.'s Office.

When he was very young, Johnny had supposed that all things in
the Office gave off the scent, the varnished chart of a man's anatomy,
the ancient, papery skull on the threelegged table in the corner, the
rows of scuffed books behind the bookcase glass, the littered desk,
the bottles on the shelves, the tree engraving, and T. D. himself.
But later he knew that the scent was from the bottles only.

The Botanical Medicines in the square glass-stoppered bottles
were made by T. D. from roots, barks, grasses, fruits, and flowers of
the County. Barkybrown, rivergreen, color of blood, they were the
bottled lifejuice of the County and the aroma of all its withered
summers.

It was in the Office, oddly appendent to the house itself, that

Johnny had come closest to the buried secret of his father's life.

One day when he was about ten years old, he had gone into the Office during his father's absence and had found lying on the desk a ledger that T. D. had always before kept carefully locked up and to which he referred for purposes that Johnny had never understood. Now, Johnny picked up the ledger and read on the outside

BOOK OF MISCELLANIES

T. D. SHAWNESSY

Inside, Johnny found many strange things. The whole first part of the book contained recipes for the Botanical Medicines. One read:

An Indian Remmady. Cure for Ague Cakes.

Take of the bark of black Haw Root Wild Cherry Root Bitter Sweet Root and Skunk Root of each one hand full put in one gallon of soft water and boil down to one quart. To be drank in one day, and so continue making and drinking for severl days if necessary.

Another:

Take of Gambage	— 2 oz
Blood-Root	— 2 oz
Labelia Seeds	— 1 oz
Cayenne pepper	— 2 drams
Rhubarb	— 4 drams
Penlash	— 1 dram

All made fine well mixed and formed into pills with butternut syrup. Dose—take one every hour—until they purg or take 4 and they will puke.

There followed many testimonials of people who had been cured by the Botanical Medicines. One read:

This may certify to all whome it may concern that I David Farnsworth of the County of Raintree in the State of Indiana have ben for years subject to repeted attacts of the pleurecy and have ben brought (as I and others have thought) very near the gates of death.

In April of 1822 I had another attact of this distressing and painful complaint. I was taken on Satterday with cold chills and flashes of heat with pains in my bones and headach and a severe pain in my

left side, with other disagreeable symtoms which continued until mon-
day with increasing rapidity, when I sent for T. D. Shawnessy to cum
and bring with him sum medicines and when he had examened me he
stated that I had better be taken through a corse of medicine without
delay. Prepperation was made and I began to drink of the hot medicine to rase the internel heat. I was then steemed, and an emettic
of Labelia with its appendents was afterwards administered and then
steemed again and showered with cold water and vinnegar then wiped
off dry and put to bed with a warm rock to my feet still drinking of
the warm teas to keep up a perspiration and by the blessing of kind
providence through the means of those medicines administered and
good nursing I was soon restored to health, and will further add that
I never was cured in so short a time of so vilent atact of this complaint. My family has also used his medicine in other complaints and
find them to answer the purpose in all cases and are so well convinced
of their suppererorety over those used by the medical docters that they
seek for no other then the Botanical Medicines.

DANIEL FARNSWORTH
ELIZABETH FARNSWORTH

August 5th, 1822

Farther over in the book were some original poems—hymns and
moral diatribes. One poem, inserted on a separate sheet of paper,
had been written in purple ink, and although it was in T. D.'s hand,
the letters were more carefully formed than usual and the capitals
had ornamental flourishes. It seemed to Johnny perhaps a hymn—
but a strange one.

> It was a morning in the Spring.
>   Beneeth a hawthorn tree we lade,
> Drunk with the od'rous blosoming,
>   Togather, kissing in the shade.
>   Heaven! how lustily we played!
>
> It was a day of frollic wind.
>   We heard the insecks drone and buz.
> God's purest angle would have sinned
>   And i, no angle, did becaus
>   My God! how bewtifull she was!
>
> It was a morning in the prime.
>   I struv the bewteus prize to win,

And if our gaming was a crime,
And if our luving was a sin,
Dear Jesus! let me err agin!

On a few pages in the back of the book were recorded some
baffling particulars about the Shawnessy family tree. One entry read:

Eliza Shawnessy, mother of Timothy Duff Shawnessy, came from
Scotland to the State of Delaware in 1805 and departed this life in
1820 at the age of forty-six.

Fair from my natif place
A strainger in this Land was I.
I go to my eturnel rest
And shall live no more to die.
From Scottish earth I came to this.
From here I go to endless bliss.

There was no mention of a Grandfather Shawnessy. Johnny knew
that T. D. had come over from Scotland with his mother when he
was a boy. T. D. would say only that his own father had 'passed
on' before mother and son had left Scotland. But there must have
been an interesting family connection there, for when Johnny—by
far the most gifted of the children—would show a flash of precocity
in memory or expression, T. D. would say,

—Well, the boy ought to amount to something some day. He's
related on my father's side to one of the greatest living writers of
the English language. Some day maybe he will make the name of
Shawnessy as great in America as the name of Carlyle has become
in England.

Then T. D.'s blue eyes would flash, his thin shoulders would
snap back, and he would walk rapidly back and forth, coattails flapping, showing the restless energy that had brought him all the way
from Scotland to the middle of America.

T. D. himself was a famous man in Raintree County. Whether
driving about with a buggyload of the Botanical Medicines or standing in the pulpit of the Methodist Church in Danwebster, rocking
back on his heels, he had but one aim—to improve the spiritual and
physical welfare of the County. Devoid equally of grammar and
guile, he had become known beyond the borders of the County for
his sermons, which were sometimes composed in spirited doggerel.

He got continual requests from other parts of the State for his poems, especially the one about the Evils of Tobacco, which Johnny had heard so many times that he knew it by heart, including the two celebrated lines:

> Some do it chew and some it smoke
> Whilst some it up their nose do poke.

There was no special mystery about this everyday T. D., but Johnny was always discovering secrets where no one else could and was endlessly curious about the origin of things and their occult relationships to one another. For him the mystery of his father's origin and his own was signed and sealed into a ledger of recipes and poems and into a legend of a tree of golden rain.

T. D. Shawnessy, his father, was a tall tree with a golden top, the carrier of a strange seed from the East planted deep in Raintree County. That was why a tree with a black legend beneath, taken from the Bible, grew in the little shrinelike office. T. D. Shawnessy was a tall, windshaken tree of life, and from the branches and the leaves thereof was a healing balsam shaken on the minds and bodies of men. And the seed of this tree had fallen on the County in secret for many years, but none there was who could say the place and the purpose and the meaning thereof.

There was also the secret of his mother, Ellen Shawnessy. His earliest memories, archaic fragments saved out of otherwise razed eras of his life, were all pervaded with the presence of his mother. These memories appeared to have been plucked out of an eternal summer and preserved by an access of strong light that burned the images more lastingly on his awareness. Perhaps the oldest memory of all was one of his mother's face bending down to him from a vague tumult of sound and color. Painted by the strong light, it was a slender face, the cheek and jawlines emphatic, the skin fair but freckled, the nose pert, the mouth large and mobile, the eyes a vivid blue in dark lashes, the hair a dark, smouldering mass. A smile suffused this precise small face with beauty and warmth. The lips moved; there was a sound, beautiful and talismanic,

—Johnny!

With this word, spoken in his mother's quick, girlish voice, he had been called from the murmurous world where he had been lulled so long in the prehistoric age before there was any Raintree County. Thus his origin was a kind of virgin birth, as if a word had touched him into being.

Later it never ceased to disturb him that he had been a somewhat belated accident in his mother's life, the last of nine children.

Ellen was universally beloved in the County, more so even than T. D., who, because he was a Methodist minister and an advocate of reform, stirred up antagonisms. In both manner and appearance she had a young charm that made her more like an older sister than a typical Raintree County mother. She was quick to laugh and joke, having an infectious gaiety lacking in T. D.'s amiable but unhumorous nature. Her enjoyments were spontaneous like a child's, and it was always fun to go with her to one of the typical Raintree County gatherings—family reunions, Saturdays at the Court House Square, church picnics, ice cream socials, patriotic celebrations. She entered into the pastimes of the younger people, even played at the running games. It was a common saying in the County that Johnny had got his great fleetness of foot from his mother. Men would say,

—When your mother first come to this county, son, she could outfoot most of the men.

Among the fairest images of his life were the occasions when Ellen Shawnessy would take some younger person's challenge to a footrace and sitting down would slip off her shoes and stockings. With shyness and wonder, Johnny saw the white feet, slender and elfin, appear suddenly where he was accustomed to see the prim-buckled shoes.

Ellen was also an excellent horsewoman, never bothering to saddle a horse but jumping on like a man and riding away bareback. This she often did, leaving at a moment's notice for the home of a friend or relative. In the supreme emergencies of life—childbirth, marriage, death—she was as much in demand as T. D., her small radiant person arriving like an omen of good luck and good hope.

Together she and T. D. were like two invulnerable angels as they went about the County dealing in life and death.

One of Johnny's most poignant early memories was of standing in the yard of the Home Place waiting for Ellen Shawnessy to come back from one of her sudden missions at a distant home. The girls had prepared both dinner and supper and had left Johnny to his own devices. He heard the talking from time to time in the house and yard.

—I wonder what can be keeping Mamma so long.

It was nearly nightfall. He couldn't remember when she had stayed away so long. He walked back and forth before the gate, looking east along the road in the direction she had taken. He had never before felt so miserable and lonely. The house, the fields surrounding, and the road had lost all purpose and significance, seeming empty and forlorn at the top of the world. At last, in the fading day, he saw Ellen's erect form riding swiftly up the road. He ran from the gate, his voice shrill:

—Mamma! Mamma! It's me—Johnny!

She rode up to him and leaped lightly off the horse, her face flushed, her hair blown and tangled.

—Why, Johnny! she said. Why haven't you gone to bed?

He was very happy to walk with her into the house and see the usual bustle and excitement on her arrival as she began to tell in her fast, crowded speech some narrative of birth, of life hanging by a thread, of what people said out there in the limitless, enchanted world of Raintree County.

His mother's being was woven into the substance of his surroundings, unchanging essence of a changing earth. There had been two distinct Home Places. Johnny's first memories preserved the earlier Home Place, the pioneer Shawnessy dwelling in Raintree County. The central shrine had been the log cabin, a sturdy, competent dwelling well floored and chinked, with two partitions downstairs and a loft above for sleeping. Behind the cabin were T. D.'s office, an outhouse, and the small barn where a few horses and cows were kept: T. D. wasn't primarily a farmer and had only twenty acres of land. Some distance from the house was a spring welling up from a small rocky hollow to form a trickling branch that made its way circuitously across the field and northward to the river. Back of the house was the main pasture, the South Field, its grassy undulations strewn with firescarred rocks, negligent droppings of some condorwinged bird of time in the ages before the first human beings had come to Raintree County. The South Field rose to a gentle summit behind the Home Place and then fell like a wave of waning strength to the limit of the Shawnessy earth. There, just inside the railfence, was the greatest of the glacial boulders, a rock much taller than Johnny, egg-shaped, faintly red, half sunken in the earth, immovable and lonely. Beyond it was the oak forest, a place of tranquil and great trunks. Johnny could remember when the South Field was stubbled with stumps, having been, some years before his birth, part of the great oak forest which apparently had covered several square miles of the land around the Home Place when T. D. first came to the County, being itself a remnant of that legendary great forest which extended clear across the Mississippi Valley and of which there were still some dim recollections handed down from the earliest settlers and explorers.

In this simple setting of cabin, road, railfences, pasturefield, corn-land, forest, spring and branch, the infant Johnny Shawnessy had grown up. Then one day in his ninth year, the family returned from a Saturday on the Court House Square to find the log cabin in flames. From its ashes rose the new Home Place, a plain board farmhouse built in the fashion of the middle forties. Slowly, too, the land lost its raw unfinished look. New outbuildings and a larger barn were built. The farm was entirely fenced in. The road was widened and corduroyed.

But under the thin veil of the new Home Place, under the tidal rhythm of the seasons, Johnny seemed always to be trying to remember and restore a pattern primitive and simple, of which only tantalizing traces remained.

Once in his tenth year he went a long way back of the land and entered the great oak forest and walked a long way through its druid aisles, wondering if he might not find in it somewhere the fabulous Raintree. He stayed longer away than he had intended. Darkness came suddenly among the broad trunks, which even at noon were steeped in a kind of twilight. He hurried back through expiring noises of the day. It seemed to him that he was going much farther than necessary to find the railfence at the limit of the land. A feeling possessed him of the fragility of his life on the earth and of the transiency of all human habitation. He had a sensation of long absence and return, or as if he had reawakened into some earlier time. Suppose he should come out of the forest and find the Home Place as it was in its early and now all but forgotten form. Nay, suppose it wasn't there at all, the road, the railfence, and the log cabin having been erased by the backward-travelling years. The primeval forest might extend once more in majestic solitude all over the lost earth of Raintree County. He was suddenly afraid, uprooted from his familiar world. He ran like mad between the trees, lashed by branches and weeds.

Abruptly, he came out at the railfence. The rock was there, faintly red in the declining light. He sprang over the fence and ran up the slow bulge of the field. Below him, across the long earth, were the yellow windows of the Home Place. A bell sounded, calling for supper. It was not so late as he had thought. His small fleet legs found a new strength. He ran on slow, floating strides down the slow hill watching for his mother's form across the land.

He then dimly understood that every memory of his life, like every journey of his body, returned at last to the same mysterious place which had nothing to do with space. And he wondered at the miracle by which he had been spun out of the substance of his mother's flesh in some prehistoric era that had nothing to do with time. Somehow he had sprung without a pollution into the world of names. And the names made all the difference and rescued him from the feeling of being lost in a void of earth and night—the names, the omnipotent words, Johnny, father, mother, Raintree County.

For Johnny always had a curious feeling that he would one day find the meaning of himself and Raintree County locked up in words. He himself had sprung into being from words in an immense blackbordered book on the parlor table.

This book was the Family Bible. On its first page the beginning of all things was recorded in the inspired word of God. On its last page Johnny's beginning was recorded in T. D.'s handwriting:

John Wickliff Shawnessy, Borned in Raintree
County at the Home Place, April 23, 1839

It early seemed to Johnny that his whole life had been woven from the pages of this august book. Over and over, at church and in the home, he heard its stories of beginnings, its dreadful dooms, and its beautiful lives and deaths. His very substance was shaped from its archaic language. In a way, even his Christian name had come from the Bible. T. D. had called his last child after the great English Reformer who had been one of the first to attempt a translation of the

Bible into English. The name, variously spelled and misspelled in the old texts, was further misspelled 'Wickliff' by T. D., and Wickliff it became in the middle of Johnny's name.

John Wickliff—this name had been set upon him like a badge. Perhaps he too was fated to rewrite the great book of God in a new land and in a new tongue.

Some of the legends of the Bible became as much a part of him as his own life in the County. His mother had early read him the story of Adam and Eve and the Garden of Eden, of God and the guileful Serpent, and of the Tree that bore the Forbidden Fruit.

The story of Adam and Eve was the oldest story in the world, sealed with the seal of primal mystery. What earth was more secret than the Garden of Eden? Where was this garden in which the father and mother of mankind had wandered naked? At first, Johnny had supposed that because Raintree County was the whole world, therefore Eden was somewhere in Raintree County, especially since there was a lake in the center of the County called Paradise Lake. But T. D. laughed pleasantly at this misconception and cleared it up.

The greatest mystery of all was the Forbidden Tree. What kind of tree was it and why was it forbidden? And where was that other tree, the Tree of Life, that Adam and Eve might also have eaten of to live forever? And why had God forbidden them to eat the fruit of the trees at all?

Yes, that story had a light of dawn like an early memory of the County. Much of the mystery came from the fact that Adam and Eve were the only people who lived naked. He had seen a picture of them in the frontispiece of the Family Bible, tasting the Forbidden Fruit, Eve having her long hair down and a figleaf over the vital spot. This story was the boldest and truest of all the stories and the most marvellous and exciting because in it the father and mother of mankind had been naked. And the wonderful word 'naked' was used, and it meant 'without clothes.'

In the Danwebster Church, where T. D. preached about God and the Bible, everyone wore clothes, a mysterious result of the sin which Adam and Eve had committed in the garden. The divine disease of curiosity that burned in the vitals of Johnny Shawnessy ended for most Raintree County citizens when they entered the church. To it they came for the same answer to life's riddle that had been given to their fathers before them.

One of the dominant images of Johnny's childhood was the approach to the Danwebster Church. Following the road from the Home Place, the family wagon would make a sharp turn, dip down through trees across the river bridge, and clattering over and through the screening foliage on the far side, would bring suddenly into view the form of the Danwebster Church standing on a hill above the river, a white frame building with a steeple holding a bell. It was like a revelation austere and tranquil. The doors would open, and the bell would ring, and from miles around the dwellers of Raintree County would gather to raise their voices in song and prayer.

What was the thing to which they prayed?

It was a rather appalling mystery called God. Toward the little church of Danwebster, Johnny had a divided emotion. He always associated it with sunshine, a gentle boredom, the image of T. D. pleasantly rocking in the pulpit. But over it there hovered too the memory of a crime, the old unlucky error by which the history of mankind had been darkened. The mystery of Raintree County was all stained and bloody and confused with this crime. The whole mournful affair was only slightly relieved by the worship of God's gentle son, who, after all, had been nailed to a cross for being good.

More satisfying to Johnny's yearning for definite answers was the little schoolhouse at Danwebster where he learned to read and write and cipher. Here he studied a legend called American History, bloody, irrational, and exciting like the Bible, and was told that he lived in the greatest republic since the beginning of time, a place where all men were created equal and where they were all entitled to Life, Liberty, and the Pursuit of Happiness. Though the school at Danwebster was only spasmodically in operation under a succession of itinerant teachers, Johnny here began to show his phenomenal memory. In Class Day exercises he recited gems of oratory and rhetoric, including the peroration of Webster's famous reply to Hayne. He emerged from his schooling with the conviction that Liberty and Union were one and inseparable, that George Washington was the greatest man who ever lived, and that two plus two equalled four in Raintree County and throughout the universe. Above all, he acquired a holy faith in the printed word.

After he had learned to read, Johnny read newspapers, books, magazines, or just odd pieces of anything covered with words. He believed that some day, if he read fast and far enough, he would strip away the thin black veil of words and behold the great mystery that dwelt at the beginning of himself. He read with complete absorption, and when he was lost in a book, he was truly and completely lost, so much so that sometimes his mother was obliged to call several times before he heard.

And as he read and didn't find the answer to the secret, he made a resolution that he would someday write the book that would unlock the riddle of the earth of Raintree County, of his mother and father, and himself. Thus when he was very young, only about seven years old, he decided upon his life work.

Most of the words that he read as a boy only carried him farther from the secret, but a few stories were filled with revelation.

In the summer of 1852, T. D. got hold of a two-volume copy of the novel *Uncle Tom's Cabin* by Harriet Beecher Stowe. He gave sermons about it, and people discussed it for weeks pro and con. It was one of the great spiritual events of Raintree County, having as much effect on the County's mind as a National Election or even a minor war. Long after Johnny had read the book, a permanent residue of simple images remained, and this residue was the great American legend of Uncle Tom's Cabin.

The legend of Uncle Tom's Cabin was a legend of the South, but not the South which was below the Ohio River, a hundred and fifty miles from Johnny's home in Indiana. It was the South of Stephen Foster's songs. It was way down upon the Swanee Ribber, far far away in the Old Kentucky Home. There beneath a scented beauty lay a black evil called slavery. There the good and the poor and the humble and the enslaved of the earth were set clearly apart by God in black skins and patiently awaited their deliverance. Uncle Tom's Cabin was the story of a few enduring characters, too simple to be real and thus more true than life: little Eva, that good, goldenhaired child, destroyed somehow by the noxious blight of slavery:

> Farewell, beloved child! the bright eternal doors have closed after thee; we shall see thy sweet face no more. . . .

Eliza running across the icefloes on the river from slave land into free with the bloodhounds roaring after; Topsy, the puckish Negro child who wasn't born but just growed; Simon Legree, whose fist had got hard as iron from knocking down niggers; and Uncle Tom himself, the good old woollytopped Negro, who died like Christ that a people might be saved.

> Think of your freedom, every time you see UNCLE TOM'S CABIN; and let it be a memorial to put you all in mind to follow in his steps, and be as honest and faithful and Christian as he was.

Uncle Tom's Cabin was a legend eternally true because it was eternally good. It spoke directly to the heart of Johnny Shawnessy and became blended in his being with Raintree County and America. After he read *Uncle Tom's Cabin,* he was never confused again about the question of slavery. He knew where and what slavery was, he knew that it was bad, he knew also that it would one day be destroyed.

There was a time during which Johnny read and reread all the Greek myths he could get hold of. It seemed to him that in these stories of human forms woven from the teeming earth, of women flying from the love-pursuit of gods beside the river, of monsters that mingled beast and god, of combat, love, and epic quests and everlasting godlike games, he had perhaps recovered the lost prehistoric summer of his own life.

At about the same time he read some of the stories of Nathaniel Hawthorne, the great American mythmaker. One of these filled him again with the old sense of mystery and seemed to have a special meaning for his own life. This was the story of 'The Great Stone Face.' Johnny read it over and over until he had it almost by heart. The austere language seemed imbued with a mystical meaning beyond the literal phrase. To him it seemed the most wonderful story ever told.

The story opened with a description of a mother and a little child named Ernest sitting at their cottage door and gazing at a Great Stone Face. High above the populous valley where they lived, a colossal face of stone had been shaped in a cliff by some remote convulsion of the earth and transformed to human aspect by the weathering touch of time. *It was a happy lot for children to grow up to manhood or womanhood with the Great Stone Face before their eyes, for all the features were noble, and the expression was at once grand and sweet, as if it were the glow of a vast, warm heart, that embraced all mankind in its affections.* Gazing at the Great Stone Face, the mother repeated to the little child a legend of the valley, older even than the Indian peoples who had formerly lived there. The purport was that some day a child would be born in the valley who would become *the greatest and noblest personage of his time,* and whose face in manhood would bear an exact resemblance to the Great Stone Face.

The boy Ernest grew up in the valley, having no teacher except the Great Stone Face. While he was yet a child, *an exceedingly rich merchant* returned to the valley, hailed as the one who fulfilled the ancient prophecy. He had great wealth and was known by the name of Gathergold. As the rich man passed in his carriage among the applauding people, Ernest caught a glimpse of a withered yellow face that bore no resemblance at all to the Great Stone Face, having none of its benignity and wisdom. And yet the people seemed actually to believe that here was the likeness of the Great Stone Face.

But as time passed, the episode was forgotten, and Ernest growing now to manhood continued to hope that he might live to see the fulfillment of the prophecy. Then there came back to the valley of his birth *an illustrious commander,* who was affectionately called Old Blood-and-Thunder and who the people asserted was the exact likeness of the Great Stone Face. Obtaining a view of the famous soldier, Ernest beheld *a war-worn and weather-beaten countenance, full of energy, and expressive of an iron will,* but lacking the gentle wisdom and humane sympathy of the Great Stone Face.

Years passed. Ernest became a preacher, remaining in the valley and hoping that he might yet see the man who would resemble the beloved Face. Then there came back to the valley of his birth *a certain eminent statesman,* who was so wonderfully eloquent that he had *finally persuaded his countrymen to select him for the Presidency.* He was known by the name of Old Stony Phiz, so much was he thought to resemble the Great Stone Face, but once again Ernest was disappointed.

Ernest was now aged and had ceased to be obscure. Meanwhile, *a bountiful Providence had granted a new poet to this earth.* Likewise a native of the valley, he had spent most of his life *a distance*

*from that romantic region, pouring out his sweet music amid the bus-
tle and din of cities.* Now he took passage by railroad and returned
to the valley in order to speak with Ernest, because he deemed nothing so desirable as to meet this man, *whose untaught wisdom walked
hand in hand with the noble simplicity of his life* and *who made
great truths so familiar by his simple utterance of them.* Ernest hoped
that the poet would fulfill the prophecy, but the poet himself declined
the nomination, insisting that while he had dreamed great dreams,
he had lived by his own choice among poor and mean realities.

Then at the story's end, Ernest had gone out to address the people,
and the light of the setting sun had shone for a brief while in mist
and splendor on the distant image of the Great Stone Face. And the
poet had called out:

*'Behold! Behold! Ernest is himself the likeness of the Great
Stone Face!'. . .*

*But Ernest, having finished what he had to say, took the poet's
arm, and walked slowly homeward, still hoping that some wiser and
better man than himself would by and by appear, bearing a resemblance to the GREAT STONE FACE.*

Here was the secret that Johnny Shawnessy was hunting. In this
story the earth itself acquired the mystical dimensions of a human
face. An ideal being appeared in distant splendor above the valley
of human years. Here was the meaning of man's aspiration woven
into the very substance of the earth.

His sensation on first reading this famous American fable was
much like the thrill he felt when he went one day into an office of
the Court House with T. D. and saw hanging on the wall a map of
Raintree County, colored and varnished, like the human anatomy in
T. D.'s Office. It was the first time he had seen a map of his home
earth, and he had a Columbian moment of discovery. The earth acquired shape, coherence, meaning. The road travelling before his
house joined other roads, was part of an integrated system. The river
coiled like the body of a snake, cutting from corner to corner of the
County. The lake was a pool of green concentric circles in the very
center of the County.

He had suddenly achieved a world. The dearly bought victory of
man over the increate and stubborn earth was his. He had gazed at
a map of his own life, the pattern of himself, securely bounded by

the four walls of Raintree County. He held the whole great riddle in the focus of his eyes—naked, imminent, perfect.

He left the Court House feeling that he had almost discovered the eternal meaning buried in the debris of all his memories, in the changing seasons of Raintree County, in the streamdivided earth, in the faces of his father and mother, and in his own elusive self that had wandered out from the brightness of an everlasting summer and hunted for itself across the everlasting earth.

And so Johnny Shawnessy passed through the years of his childhood steeping himself in legends old and new. From this preoccupation came a dream that he dreamed repeatedly just before awakening and which he relinquished always with an emotion of regret. The dream itself was apparently the memory of a dream, an archetypal dream; perhaps that was why it was always much the same.

Dreaming, he was trying to recover the memory of a sacred place. He couldn't remember now in what summer he had been there. He must have been a child, though he had possessed vigor and desire more than a child's. He remembered only vaguely the temple whose circular roof was open to the summer so that the tree within might live. For a long time, he had possessed a golden bough and had meant to keep it for a token, all heavy with seed and fruit. He could not even remember the face of one whom he had known there in that tranquil summer. She had been beautiful, and, yes, assuredly, his desire had been more than a child's. And were not the morals of that maternal deity delightfully suspect? He had even forgotten all the names—the names equally of the tree, the goddess, and the shrine, the singular names which he knew he must have heard over and over. He had forgotten the name of the curious and curving pathway to the place. And he had even forgotten his own name, the special name that they had given him because he was the only one who had found the way. He had been amazed by the vast extent of the forest around him, the immense and silent grove steeped in twilight, through which weak sunrays filtering fell, and he remembered the distant and soft floor of the forest, and the trunks of trees, all oaks of an extinct species. Through that forest he had walked, and in its shadow he had lived, and there he had discovered the place of sacred waters. But then all this must have been a memory of something he had read or heard. If only once again he might return and

stand where the slant rays touched with fire the topmost branches of
the tree! Then perhaps a golden warmth would descend his body,
and he would discover in the twilight of the trunk a goddess exquisitely formed, whose gold hair lay along the earth and whose precise face would stir him to recognition. Then perhaps he would
recapture the word which had been from the beginning, which had
awakened him from sleep and touched his ears with music and ec-
stasy, a word that quivered through the grove

AND CAUSED THE TREE TO SHIVER AND SEND DOWN
A RAIN OF YELLOW AND
UNUSUAL

Dust bloomed and drifted from President's hooves as the surrey drew abreast of the Old Home Place and went by without stopping. Distant explosions, linked and separate, began to intrude through the steady noise of hooves and wheels.

—Listen to them in town, Wesley said.

—We could always hear them on the Fourth from here, Mr. Shawnessy said.

—Was the Fourth any fun when you were a boy, Papa?

—It was a good Fourth. We took it even harder than you do today. We usually went into Freehaven early in the morning. Of course, the town was very different then. The Old Court House was there then and——

—What happened to it? Wesley asked.

—It burned down during the Civil War.

—What was it like?

—Well, it was a rather plain brick building, not nearly so big as the present court house. It was a rectangle in shape with some white wooden columns in front, Southern style, and a little wooden cupola.

—Did it have a clock and a flag?

—A flag, yes. But no clock.

Mr. Shawnessy remembered the Old Court House. It stood soft and clear in the air of a remembered summer, the young earth of Raintree County was beneath it, the ancient buildings of the Square enclosed it, the Court House Square was filled with people, the fronts of stores were gay with bunting, firecrackers burst. And the Old Court House was there, a flag was flying from the cupola, but there was no clock to tell the time of day.

The surrey was well past the Old Home Place. He could see the treebordered fringe of the Shawmucky, where the road made its immemorial jog and straightened out for the run into Freehaven.

Listen, it was all a dream, I know, of the Great War and of growing older and of all the faces of the children. The river crosses there under the bridge, the road jogs, firecrackers are crumping in the distant morning.

I must hurry down the road to the County Seat. I must hurry through the young morning of America. I must be there early and walk ceaselessly around the clockless Court House. I must press my eager young face close to the faces of the crowd. I must see my young tousled head reflected in the store windows. I must also go somewhere and get something hot and strong to eat.

I must find you there, too. I must look wistfully from a distance at your little puritan face with freckles on it. I must hunt you out in the strong light of the Court House Square. I shall not look you straight in the eye and say, I love you, because you will be taller than I.

In the Court House Square, the vender of tonics bestows lush and fragrant locks on all the true believers. The Professor puts his pointer to the Phrenological Chart. The band plays 'Yankee Doodle,' and a small boy sets off a big cracker under the Speaker of the Day.

In the Court House Square, the athlete stands with cocked arms bulging. By God, he will run any man in the County! By God, none shall beat him!

But I will walk swiftly and ceaselessly in the fringes of the crowd. My faunlike being shall be woven through the fabric of the crowd. They shall not any of them die or change.

And somewhere in the crowd, the harshvoiced, fierce, exciting crowd, I shall walk holding the little black book in which my name is written. And I shall hear words spoken in the Square, thin syllables of vanished summers, I shall hear the words before the words became Events, before the words became History. I didn't know it then, but the words were really the seeds of battles and of marches, the words were also love that is a shy flower opening beside remembered waters, the words were also dead men lying in the rain, bloated bodies between the cornrows in the beautiful July earth of America. I didn't know it then, but the words were seeds, falling at random in the Court House Square, falling through the summer air of Raintree County, and the strange fruit of the little seeding words was always love and death. But now I must hasten to the Square, for in Freehaven it is the Fourth of July, they are hanging out the flag with one and thirty stars, the band is playing 'Yankee Doodle' for

BIG CROWD OF PEOPLE
HAD POURED INTO THE COURT HOUSE SQUARE

of Freehaven for the Fourth of July Celebration. Among them was Johnny Shawnessy, fifteen years old, bony and angular and beginning to bust out of his kneepants. His head looked too big for his body, his hair was a tangled mat of brightness, his cheeks and chin showed the beginnings of a beard and were sprinkled with little pimples. From a platform erected on the court house yard, a military band blasted out number after number, while the people came streaming from every corner of the County, into the foursided, sunflooded morning of the Square. There they walked with shining eyes, looking over their shoulders, craning their necks, bobbing out from behind buildings as if they were hunting for something.

Johnny Shawnessy was hunting for something too. Whenever he came to the Court House Square on festive days, he vaguely hoped for two things: that he would stand before the crowd a hero and be rocked with a thunder of hands; and that he would find in the crowd a lovely girl he had never seen before, who, perceiving at once his great soul through the callow veil of his fifteen years, would go with him to a place remote from the crowd, where she would take off her dress and all her petticoats for him, and he would be her impetuous lover, kneepants and all.

—Hello, Johnny.

The name was said in a manner softly personal. He turned around. A strange girl, half a head taller than he, was standing on the sidewalk with a boy he had never seen before.

—Nell!

Johnny hadn't seen Nell Gaither for years. When he was much smaller, he had gone to school with her and had seen her often at the Danwebster Church with her father and mother. Mrs. Gaither had been a fragile, lovely woman from a Connecticut family of means and culture. She had come with her husband in the great migration West, and they had settled in Raintree County in the late thirties to

the hard existence of making a living from the earth. Nell had been
the first child, and for a long time the only one. Johnny remembered
how Nell had always seemed so much more ladylike than the other
girls he knew, probably because of her mother's influence. Then
when Nell was seven, Mrs. Gaither had died after the birth of a still-
born child, and Mr. Gaither had sent the girl back to her mother's
family in the East. And that was the last Johnny had heard of her
until now.

—Where did you come from, Nell? he asked.

—I'm back with Daddy, Nell said. He's married again, you know,
and I'm going to live here for a while. O, by the way, Johnny, I want
you to meet a friend of mine, Garwood Jones.

Garwood Jones was a large, sleek, florid boy, perhaps a year older
than Johnny. He had a broad, smooth face, dark, wavy hair fragrant
with oil, and blue eyes filled with faint amusement. He thrust out
his hand and said in an incredibly big voice,

—Happy to make your acquaintance, John.

The greeting was both personal and patronizing.

—Pleased to meet you, Johnny said.

—What part of the County are you from, John?

Johnny told him, and the boy said that he used to live at Waycross
in the southeast corner but that his family had long ago moved to
Freehaven.

—Garwood is speaking on the program today, Johnny, Nell said.

—Just a few patriotic recitations, the boy said with arrogant
humility.

Johnny didn't dislike Garwood Jones, but he envied the smooth,
newly razored face, the deep voice, the long trousers, and the place
on the Program of the Day.

—How did you and Nell get to know each other? Johnny said.

—O, I get to know all the pretty girls, John, Garwood said.

He laughed a throaty laugh. The flat of his hand fell affectionately between Johnny's shoulderblades.

In the old days, Johnny had never thought of Nell as especially
pretty. Now he looked at her a little more closely. The thin, serious
child was gone. Nell had her hair bound up like a woman's, showing
her long white neck. A sort of small crazy hat teetered on her sun-
colored curls. Her face, which was rather small, was studiedly se-

rene, the chin held high, the unusual, fleshy mouth primly closed. The very wide-apart green eyes, her most attractive feature, looked calmly down at him a little sideways past her nose, which was pert and covered with freckles. She had on a white shortsleeved dress. She had the steep breasts of a budding girl and was getting somewhat wide in the hips, although her waist was very slender and her arms were long, angular, and childlike.

She stood, right hand on hip and left hand over right hand, dangling a parasol, while her left foot was toed out to show her new shoe.

Johnny thought she looked a little dowdy and ridiculous, but when she spoke, her voice was very husky, grave, and sweet. He noticed especially the soft, personal way in which she said his name, as if she had practiced it.

—I'll see you at church, Sunday, Johnny, she said.

The small lofty face smiled. Nell suddenly shot her parasol open. The interview was at an end.

—Well, John, Garwood Jones said, I trust I will have the pleasure of seeing you again.

He removed his straw hat and made a stately bow, and he and Nell walked away toward a lemonade stand. Johnny stood watching Nell walk, her hips softly moving as if revolving around a center, while her long, slender back and primly held shoulders were motionless.

—Hey, Johnny!

His brother Zeke was waving from in front of the Saloon. In the middle of a crowd there, a young man stood, white teeth flashing from a brown bearded face. In one hand he held a beermug, and with the other he kept pushing back the brown shag of his hair. His skintight pants showed off the hard length of his legs and the great breadth of his whiteshirted chest and shoulders. The young man laughed and said in a harsh, high voice, as Johnny approached,

—I can beat any man or boy in the County, and here's five dollars says I can.

He buried his white teeth in the mug and came up, mouth and beard shining. A gold coin glinted in his free hand. A hush fell on the crowd. Two men removed their hats, perhaps to see better. Johnny joined Zeke on the edges of the crowd.

—I said I can lick any man or boy in this County.

—And he can do it too, a solemn, sharpfaced man confided to Johnny. Just like he says, can't none of 'em touch 'im. Flash Perkins kin outrun 'em all.

From this remark, Johnny gathered that the talk was about the annual Fourth of July Footrace by which the fastest runner in Raintree County was determined.

—Our boy from Prairie Township'll make yuh eat them words this afternoon, a voice in the crowd said.

—Who said that? Flash Perkins said.

His forehead shot up into ridges, his mouth went on smiling, his eyes never changed from the childlike, excited look. He shoved his way into the crowd.

—Hot darn! Zeke said. A fight!

The crowd withdrew leaving one man alone in a ring of red faces. The man, a tall gawky fellow, looked embarrassed and put upon. He extended his arm, his finger almost touching Flash Perkins' nose.

—Take it easy now, brother, he said. Better not start nothin' you cain't finish.

His voice was high and nervous.

—You the man that said that? Flash Perkins asked.

—Yes, I am. I said it, and I stick by it.

—Reckon you wouldn't want to cover that there statement with a little coin?

The man looked relieved.

—I cain't cover it by myself, but they's a bunch of us from Prairie will make up a pot for Pud Foster.

—Git a hat, said a voice.

—Here's a hat, said a voice.

—Who's here'll back Pud Foster from Prairie?

—I'll put in, a man said. He can beat any beersot from town any day.

Several men shoved their way in and began to talk bets. There was a frightful blast of sound. It was the band starting up again. They were playing 'Yankee Doodle.'

—Shucks, Zeke said. No fight.

—But that sure ought to be some race, Johnny said.

—What's going on, boys?

It was T. D. He was taller than anyone else in the crowd. His blond pointed beard was bobbing up and down. He was rubbing his hands together and smacking his lips.

—They're betting on a race, Johnny said.

—That's what I thought, T. D. said.

He pushed his way into the crowd.

—Gambling is a sin before the Lord, gentlemen. Put up your money.

—Put up your lip, you old she-goat, a man said.

The crowd roared.

—Pa's gittin' hisself into something, Zeke said. Looks like they might be a fight after all, and us in it.

—No harm done, Pop, Flash Perkins said. Here, give the old guy a drink.

—Who is that crazy old bastard, anyway? the solemn, sharpfaced citizen said to Zeke.

—That's my pa, Zeke said.

Zeke was seventeen and looked a man. His red hair bristled all directions.

—What's that? the man said.

—I said that's my father.

—O, the man said. Is that a fact?

He looked thoughtful and began to move away through the crowd.

—Young man, T. D. said to Flash Perkins, who was holding his beermug in one hand and a hatful of money in the other, don't you know that your body is a temple of the spirit and you defile it and pollute it with that devil's brew you have there?

Flash's forehead made ridges.

—If you say so, Pappy.

—Hello, Johnny.

It was Ellen Shawnessy, her face excited and curious, her small body straining on tiptoes to see over the shoulders of the crowd.

—What's T. D. doing? she asked.

—Pa's preaching a little at them.

T. D. went on talking awhile about the lusts of the flesh and the wages of sin. He clasped his hands behind his back in the usual way and teetered back and forth from heels to toes, smiling amiably at the crowd, his long blue eyes a little absent and noticing things that went on some distance away. His closing remarks were delivered in some haste, like a child's recitation.

—What are they betting about? Ellen whispered to Johnny.

—The Footrace, Johnny said.

—When is it?

—I don't know.

—Be sure not to let me miss it, she said.

—O.K., O.K., Reverend, I get it, Flash Perkins said. We were just foolin'.

T. D. bowed pleasantly, straightened his tie, and walked serenely down the street with Ellen. The crowd went right on arguing and making bets, only now they all moved into the Saloon and got drinks. Johnny could see through the batwing doors how they laughed and swatted each other's backs and how they kept wiping beer out of their mustaches.

—I hope he loses that race, Zeke said.

But Johnny somehow felt that Flash Perkins would win the race. He looked like the winner type.

—Ladies and Gentlemen, spare me a little of your precious time, boomed a rich voice from the court house lawn.

Behind a table loaded with brightcolored bottles, stood a man with noble black mane and heavy beard, unshorn, lustrous, magnificent.

—I trust you all perceive the object which I hold in my hand, the man said, as the boys joined the crowd.

—Yes, we see it, Perfessor.

—What is it?

—Well, what of it?

—It is nothing, the man said, but a bottle, a simple, unadorned, ordinary bottle. And yet, friends, this simple, plain, unadorned, and ordinary bottle contains in it a secret preparation, the miracle-worker of our age. Ladies and Gentlemen, may I have just a little of your precious time to describe to you the extree-ordinary virtues of the elixir contained in this bottle?

—Sure. Go on.

—Get to the point, Perfessor.

—I am getting to the point, the man said serenely, and judging, my good sir, from the condition of *your* scalp and hair, you would be wise to pay special heed to what I have to say.

The man who had said, Get to the point, was standing right beside Johnny. He was a short man, genteelly dressed. Singled out, he put his hand up and smoothed a wreath of hair fitted down on his bare dome.

—Now then, the speaker continued, I trust you will all permit me to indulge in a little personal reminiscence. I am sure that few of you will believe me when I tell you that not many years ago my head was fast approaching the condition of hairlessness that you behold in the gentleman on the front row and in several other domes which I see about me here and which are, in the words of the poet,

> Open unto the fields and to the sky,
> All bright and glittering in the smokeless air.

Now I think we will all agree that the good Lord never does anything without a purpose, and if he meant mankind to go about with his skull naked of hair, why did he bestow upon us this lush and luxuriant foliage that in our natural state starts and stands triumphantly, according to the words of the poet,

> With all its fronds in air?

Fellow Americans, the good Lord intended each and every one of us to have his hair and all of it too, for as the fellow said about his wife, She ain't much, but I mean to hang on to her if I can.

The crowd whahwhahed.

—Yes, Ladies and Gentlemen, I was once in the condition of several of you here. For about twenty years, my hair had been turning gray and had become very stiff and unpliant. Bald patches were appearing on my scalp, and the skin scaled off. Each time I brushed my hair, I found the brush matted with dry tufts of hair. I tried all the famous hair restoratives on the market, but they seemed to only aggravate my condition. Then a friend told me about Mrs. Allen's World Hair Restorer and reported to me the marvellous recoveries effected thereby. I will confess to you that I was very skeptical at first, but on the repeated importunities of my friend, I finally gave in and purchased a bottle of Mrs. Allen's World Hair Restorer. Ladies and Gentlemen, need I say more? Within a week or two, a noticeable change was apparent. My hair began to recover the black lustre it had in my younger days when a boy in the hills of western Virginia. My head became entirely clear of dandruff, and new hair grew where the old had been. You see before you today, Ladies and Gentlemen, a man whose pride and hair have been restored together and general health improved. Butler, my acquaintances often remark to me, where did you get the fine wig? But I assure you, friends, it is no wig.

—It looks like a wig to me, friend, the baldheaded man said.

—Pull it, friend, the vender said.

The baldheaded man walked right out of the crowd and carefully examined the speaker's head. He pulled hard.

—No sir, he said, that's no wig.

—You bet it isn't, the speaker said. It's hair, friend, live and lusty, and you can have a head like that too, friend.

—How can I, friend? said the baldheaded man, now standing beside the speaker.

—Very simple, friend. Purchase one bottle of Mrs. Allen's World Hair Restorer for one dollar and fifty cents, and I will personally guarantee that you will have the beginnings of a fine head of hair in a week or two.

—I'll take a bottle of that, the baldheaded man said.

He pulled out a dollar and a half and gave it to the speaker.

—And just to be sure that you get your money's worth, the speaker said, I am going to give away to you free, gratis, and for no extra charge this large bottle of Doctor Hostetter's Celebrated Stomach Waters, guaranteed to cure any and all diseases of the alimentary tract, nervous, respiratory, muscular, and circulatory systems—to wit, stomach ache, heartburn, dyspepsia, diarrhea, dysentery, dizziness, fainting spells, biliousness, piles, pimples, arthritis, lumbago, rheumatism, jaundice, kidney trouble, female complaints, and organic weaknesses caused by youthful indiscretion or the approach of old age. For the next ten minutes, to everyone who can get up here with a dollar and fifty cents, I will make this extra-special-gigantic-double-for-your-money offer of two bottles. Mrs. Allen's World Hair Restorer is also an excellent hair-dressing for the ladies.

—I'll take *two* orders, Perfessor, said the baldheaded man, who was still holding his money and had not yet got his hands on the bottle.

—Here you are, my friend, the man said.

He gave the baldheaded man four bottles and put the money in his pocket.

The baldheaded man opened a bottle of the hair-restorer, shot a little of the brown liquid into the cup of his hand, and rubbed it on his head. There was a silence. A hundred eager faces watched the little man with the shiny bald head.

—It tingles, said the baldheaded man.

—You bet it does, friend, the vender said. It tingles, and that means it's taking already. Use that bottle religiously, friend, and I predict the barbers of this community will get a lot of your money before the year is out.

—But he ain't from this community, a man next to Johnny said.

—Where's he from? another man said.

—I dunno, the first man said, but I never seen him before.

—And, said the vender, let me be the first to congratulate you on the great discovery which you have just made. Your wife will be a happy woman, friend.

—I'm not married, friend, said the baldheaded man.

—You will be, friend, you will be! said the vender magnificently. No woman in town will be able to resist you when you grow the shiny, black, and vigorous head of hair that will spring up in response to the stimulating power of this wonderful hair restorative.

Johnny Shawnessy felt happy because the baldheaded man had discovered the secret for getting back his hair; he was very happy, too, to see how people flocked up and bought bottle after bottle from the vender. He could not remember ever having seen so much money in so short a time.

—How can he make any money, giving that other bottle away? Johnny asked.

—I reckon he does it for fun, Zeke said. Look how he's enjoyed hisself.

—I wish I had a dollar and fifty cents, Johnny said. I'd like to get a couple of bottles.

—But you got all your hair, and you ain't sick, Zeke said.

—Just the same—— Johnny said.

Just then the band struck up again, and the two boys moved reluctantly away. They watched the baldheaded man withdraw from the crowd. Moving along close to this person whose scalp now seemed to shine with the promise of reviving hair, they were a little surprised when he stopped at a small tent on the other side of the Square and went in. They waited, and in a moment, he came out again, carrying a large board frame, which he hung over a nail on a maple tree beside the tent. The frame bore a huge picture of a head, seen in profile and with all the upper part, beginning on a level with the eye, divided into sections, in each of which a word was written. Some of the words were Acquisitiveness, Alimentativeness, Amativeness, Cautiousness, Sublimity, Spirituality, Self-Esteem, Approbativeness. Above the picture were the words

PROFESSOR GLADSTONE, WORLD-RENOWNED
PHRENOLOGIST.

At the bottom were the words

KNOW THYSELF.

The little man re-entered the tent and reappeared with a pointer, an armload of small clothbound books, and a cowbell, which he began to ring. A large crowd gathered.

—Allow me, said the baldheaded man, to introduce myself, Ladies and Gentlemen. I am Professor Horace Gladstone. Those of you who may have heard me lecture lately in the great city of Cincinnati will pardon me if I repeat some of the things I said there to the distinguished company which assembled in the great lecture hall of that metropolis of the West.

Now I have a question to ask each and every intelligent person gathered here. Friend, are you everything today that you would like to be? Are you as rich as you wish? Do you excel in the social graces? Do you radiate that personal magnetism which makes the great to respect you and the humble to acknowledge your superiority? Why, friends, *why* are there so many blighted and unhappy lives, so many stunted souls, so many men and women today in this great and glorious country of ours who are something less than they had hoped to be in the blithe optimism of their youth?

Ladies and Gentlemen, I can answer that question. It is through a simple ignorance of the scientific principles that regulate human life. O, you say, Perfessor, don't go giving me any high-falutin' language about science because I can't understand it. Friends, it is my happy good fortune to have it within my power to open up to each and every one of you all the marvellous secrets of a great new science, by which you can achieve, like thousands before you, complete self-knowledge and self-control. That science, Ladies and Gentlemen, is the great new science of Phrenology.

Now we all agree, do we not, that no man can or does exist in rational society without a brain. May I say that in Kentucky, whence I have lately come, I felt some disposition to modify that statement, but——

The Professor waited for the applause and laughter of the crowd to subside.

—But I see no need to do so for the intelligent and enlightened concourse that I see before my eyes. Now, we all know that the brain is the instrument of every mental act, just as every movement of the body has to be performed by a muscle. Certain areas of the brain control certain human faculties and are large or small in proportion to the development of the faculties they control. Thanks to the great experiments and studies of Professors Gall, Spurheiz, and Fowler, it is now possible to say with the strictest accuracy which part of the brain controls which faculty. These facts are now available to all. Nothing is simpler, once these principles are known, than to apply them.

I have myself become a specialist in the science of Phrenology. I have examined the heads of three Presidents and many other great and distinguished heads here and abroad, not excepting the crowned heads of Europe. By helping people to become better acquainted with their strong and weak points, I have been able to direct them to a fuller exercise or restraint of certain faculties. Many hundreds and thousands of people have already benefited from this instruction. Penniless paupers have become the possessors of uncounted pelf. Timid and backward souls have sought and won the hands of the richest and most ravishing maidens. Old men have recovered the lost joys of their juvenescence. Gentlemen and Ladies, I am here in your fair little city of Middletown——

—This ain't Middletown, said a voice in the crowd. It's Freehaven.

—Freehaven, said the Professor. Thank you, friend, for the cor-

rection. I am here in this fair little city of Freehaven for a limited time.
I have a small stock of books left over from my travels in the great
cities of the West, and I should like to get rid of them as rapidly as
I can. Now I wish I could give each and every one of you a private
and personal analysis of your phrenological faculties. Alas, my
friends, due to the small time I have at my disposal, I must forego
this signal pleasure. But I have here between my two hands a little
book that contains all the advice needful. It is perfectly within the
comprehension of every one and each of you. On the inside page of
this book is a copy of the chart which you see hanging here, and a
table of the phrenological faculties. Now the book is entirely self-
explanatory, but I am willing to give a little demonstration here of
Phrenological Analysis, if someone in the crowd will be so kind as
to volunteer.

There was a silence.

—Come, don't be embarrassed, the Professor said. It's absolutely
free of charge, and furthermore I will give to anyone who so volun-
teers for the instruction of this amiable and enlightened company
one of these books at half-price instead of the usual price of one dollar and fifty cents.

Johnny Shawnessy felt himself propelled from behind out of the
crowd. He heard Zeke laughing, and he was about to duck back, but
the Professor was tapping him smartly on the shoulder with his
pointer.

—Yes, my boy. Step right up here. I am about to do you a great
favor, my boy. O, that I had had the inestimable blessing of a
Phrenological Analysis when I was your age! How old are you, my
boy?

—Fifteen, Johnny said. I didn't mean to——

—Perfectly all right, my boy. Just come up on this platform and
sit down here on the edge of this table.

A firecracker exploded, and the band struck up a number. The
Professor waved his hands to indicate that nothing could be accomplished until the band was through. For the first time in his life,
Johnny had the sensation of being extracted from the crowd and
placed above it in naked isolation. The Court House Square was con-
verging upon him; he was being absorbed by its manifold bright
eyes. The band stopped playing.

—Ladies and Gentlemen, said the little man, we have an interesting head here, a very interesting head. To you, this may be only another head, more or less, but to the practiced eye of the phrenologist, this boy's character and potentialities—nay, his whole past, present, and future—are legible in the geography of his skull. Now, then, just cast your eyes on this chart a moment, friends, and notice this section of the head below the eye.

The pointer touched the glazed, segmented head and underlined the word LANGUAGE.

—According to phrenological principles, friends, we are to measure the degree of prominence which these various areas of the skull possess and we can determine thereby the capabilities of the person we are dealing with. Now then——

A fat hand touched moistly the region below Johnny's eyes.

—Open your eyes, boy. Don't sit there blinking like an owl.

As usual the sun hurt his eyes; there was much light in the Square.

—Extraordinary, the man said. Very.

The crowd drew closer. People gathered from far back.

—Very, very interesting. Please observe, folks. Very long eyes and set somewhat forward in the head. Cheekbones prominent. In a boy of fifteen, the development is quite unusual. Now, then, let us turn to the book.

The man expertly thumbed the book.

—Here we are. 'Such people are (I quote) exceedingly expressive in all they say and do, have a most expressive countenance, eye, and manner in everything; have a most emphatic way of saying and doing everything, and thoroughly impress the various operations of their own minds on the minds of others; use the very word required by the occasion; are intuitively grammatical, even without study, and say oratorically whatever they attempt to say at all; commit to memory by reading or hearing once or twice; learn languages with remarkable facility; are both fluent and copious, even redundant and verbose,' and so forth, and so forth.

There was a stir in the crowd.

—Here, the man said, are pictures illustrating these developments. An engraving of the great English author Charles Dickens, whose linguistic characteristics are excessively developed.

—Say. Perfessor, Zeke said from the crowd, you ain't fer wrong about that boy. He's got a head for memorizing like nothin' you ever seen.

—There you are, the little bald man said, Phrenology never lies. And I was about to say that even if the boy hadn't shown any faculty in that direction, it was high time he cultivated his natural aptitude for it. But to pass on.

The Professor went all over Johnny's head, pointing out interesting hills and hollows and putting numbers in a chart that was in the front of one of the books. Finally, the Professor had worked clear over the top of Johnny's head and down to the base of his skull behind.

—Mirthfulness, the Professor said. Very large. This boy ought to be the fiddle of the company.

—Ain't that T. D. Shawnessy's son? a man said.

—Smart little cuss, someone said.

—What a cute boy! a woman said.

The band blew up; it was another march. Everyone began talking very loud and strong. People were laughing violently. Somebody set off a firecracker under a fat man in the crowd and blew his hat off. A horse got scared and began dragging a buggy down the street. The band finished its number, and by that time the Professor had made another discovery.

—Very remarkable! the Professor said in a loud voice. For a boy of his age too. Most extree-ordinary! Unusual, to say the least.

—What is it, Perfessor?

The crowd was now participating freely in the examination.

—Let us in on it, too, Perfessor.

—Has he got lice?

—Ladies and Gentlemen, the Professor said, please observe the remarkable development of this boy's head at the base of the skull. The lump of AMATIVENESS is remarkably distended.

—What does that mean, Perfessor?

—What does that mean, friend? To put it bluntly, this young gentleman is going to be an extra-special catch for the ladies.

The Professor winked and rubbed his hands jovially together. People in the crowd sniggered. Various men felt the back of their skulls.

—Hey, girls, Zeke said, I got a lump back there big as a duck's egg.